ALSO BY RUSSELL SMITH

How Insensitive
Noise
Young Men

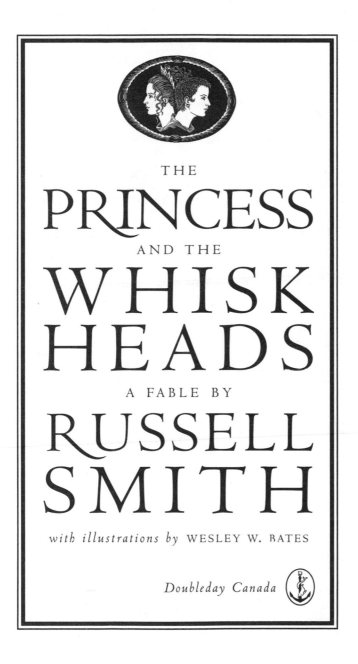

THE

PRINCESS

AND THE

WHISK
HEADS

A FABLE BY

RUSSELL
SMITH

with illustrations by WESLEY W. BATES

Doubleday Canada

Doubleday Canada and colophon are trademarks.

National Library of Canada Cataloguing in Publication Data

Smith, Russell, 1963–
The princess and the whiskheads

ISBN 0-385-65898-2

I. Bates, Wesley W. II. Title.

PS8587.M58397P74 2002   C813'.54   C2001-903599-3
PR9199.3.S553P74 2002

Jacket and text illustrations: Wesley W. Bates
Design: CS Richardson
Printed and bound in Canada

Published in Canada by
Doubleday Canada, a division of
Random House of Canada Limited

Visit Random House of Canada Limited's website: www.randomhouse.ca

FRI 10 9 8 7 6 5 4 3 2 1

For Belinda Smith

THE PRINCESS AND THE WHISKHEADS

ONE

N C E
THERE WAS
A PRINCESS WHO
RULED A TINY KINGDOM.
Which would have made her
a queen, but (I can explain)
the old king, her father, was still alive. He had officially
given the governance of the state to her because he was
too old and tired to see to the daily trivialities. So,
although her mother the queen was long dead, she was
still called Princess Juliana out of respect for her father.
Furthermore, she was so young and pretty she looked like
a princess.

The kingdom was called Liralove, and was almost
circular in shape. Bounded by a mountain range on one
side and by a high concrete wall to the north, it was pro-
tected from the cruel and contemptuous industrial state
that surrounded it. There was one city in the kingdom —
Stjornokh, the capital — and a few nearby villages; the
rest was meadows, streams, lakes, and small forests, all

dotted with the low stone houses that were an architectural tradition of the Liralovians.

They enjoyed a temperate climate: snowy in winter, warm and humid for two or three months, and misty the rest of the time. Behind each house wet green gardens flourished, filled with wildflowers, morning glories, clematis, dahlias, primroses, peonies, roses of all colours — and, as the Liralovians would proudly show you, oleander (although even the most experienced of the famous gardeners of the kingdom struggled a little with the oleander; they brought them into the warmth in winter).

The dwellings, whose gardens were separated by low stone walls, were mostly ancient, but so solid there was little need to build more — except in the capital, which was a centre of art and philosophy and was home to many bristling steel structures, fantastic architectural models without much function.

There were about a dozen of these. Intricate towers and spires, made of foreign stones, coloured glass, and finely wrought platforms of chrome and mesh striped the sky. Invisibly suspended staircases led nowhere; turrets with gleaming windows were held aloft by snaking arms; interior corridors became labyrinths. Some towers even had moving parts, and parts that made sounds in the wind: reflective shields that spun like wailing comets around the spires in the afternoon light, sheets of silky fabric that floated like hummingbirds up and down the galleries and balustrades. Some towers comprised impenetrable dark solids like building blocks, and some boasted feats of engineering that made them appear impossibly balanced, whole gridded platforms hovering high above the grey stone streets below.

These towers, known as the Architectons, built by the kingdom's most popular artists, young and old, were the fruit of a prosperous and tolerant state. They housed no lords' apartments nor merchants' offices, but were simply for marvel and discussion, pure form, the plastic manifestation of the great architects' whimsy and experimentation; rich food for stories not yet told.

The other famous Liralovian tradition was the working of jewellery with microscopically fine wire. The wire was made from precious metals — silver, gold, and platinum — beaten to airy thinness and woven into abstract shapes. These were sometimes worn as necklace or bracelet, sometimes actually woven into the skin like a metal tattoo.

This unhygienic practice was the most traditional use for the jewellery, but had fallen into disuse in the last century. In the countryside, a few ancient craftsmen still sported white beards and the traditional leather trousers of the peasant, with patterns of silver illuminating their forearms and shoulders, gleaming like a network of rivers seen from a mountainside.

The young no longer subjected themselves to the decoration. Mostly, nowadays, the jewellery was bought and sold for display, like sculpture. It was dazzlingly intricate, so fine as to disappear from sight at certain angles.

It remained in the eye only as a brief flash, an ethereal gleaming, a lacy imprint of light.

This was the kingdom's only export. Foreign artists and anthropologists were never able to duplicate the amazing delicacy of the wire lace, nor even analyze the conditions of its making: the skill was kept a close secret of the craftsmen and their women, who passed it only to their sons and daughters. Sadly, there were fewer and fewer still living who were truly skilled.

Juliana's father had amassed a fine collection of traditional work and kept it in the castle's galleries.

The castle — itself built by her family, long centuries before the vogue for Architectons — gripped a mountaintop just outside the city. It was made of a translucent rose-coloured stone, and spiky with high towers.

Juliana's private apartment looked over the city. Her favourite sight was the view from her two narrow, arched windows, through the vines that wrapped around their sills: at dusk, the tallest of the Architectons looked like a fine needle. A column of emerald stone glowed at its centre and it was wound with stairways and studded with platforms bearing sheets at odd angles like sails. In the setting sun it seemed to spin, shift, and flutter like a living thing.

The princess's days were not busy. She trusted her councillors and advisors, and the systems of administration that her father had established. She cared, of course, passionately, for her kingdom and her subjects. She knew that the talk among the noblemen, and in the

Convocation of Commoners, was of improving the sewage system in the capital, which was unsanitary; she was even prepared to donate a large sum of her own money to this project, and was trying to take an interest in the physical details of the construction plans, but this was difficult when there were so many experts who knew so much more about it than she did. She had confidence in her engineers.

She also knew that it was important to attend as many public openings and ceremonies as she could. Truth be told, there weren't many of these, so she had not often cause to take a carriage or horse down the steep hill into the capital.

But her image was everywhere in city and village: because of the public memory of her wise father and because of her youthful beauty, she was much loved by the populace. Her long red hair was especially idolized by the public sculptors.

She was fortunate to be able to spend pleasant idle time with the other children of noble families: she frequently saw the handsome Lord Lucas, who had excelled, in his adolescence, at swordplay and riding, and who had only recently studied politics for a year, abroad, at a famous progressive university, so that now he was preoccupied with social reform. He was particularly concerned with the kingdom's sewage system. He was working on a bill, to be presented at the Diet of Lords, which would institute a costly overhaul of the entire city's underground and, he claimed, improve the lot of countless poor families, now living in unpleasant and unsanitary conditions. The princess's advisors saw him as something of a romantic, as overly sensitive, perhaps even a troublemaker, but Juliana herself admired him for this new social conscience — a great improvement over endless talk of sport — and was prepared to support his bill; still she found him a little bit single-minded on the issue.

He did, of course, continue to find much time for riding and hunting with other noblemen of his age — most of whom were blond and tall, like him.

Princess Juliana's other close friend, the amusing Count Bostock, was more concerned with poetry than hunting. He had been cursed since childhood with an unnaturally curved spine, which prevented him from excelling at sports (although he had taught himself to ride passing well), and turned his interest to art and conversation. He had a sallow skin, a hooked nose, and short, spiky black hair, and he affected flamboyant clothing, some of which was even imported from foreign cities. He wore velvet jackets and ruffled shirts, whose cuffs would fly as he gestured and declaimed, laughing, with triple puns and phrases from foreign tongues. He was well acquainted with the political squabbles and artistic trends of surrounding countries, and was a great asset to any party — but the older lords and ladies worried that he would not prove much of a statesman, as he claimed to muster so little interest in the serious matters of state.

He felt nothing but amusement, for example, at

Lucas's earnest career in sewage. It must be said that this was perhaps due to some unacknowledged jealousy — Bostock saw Juliana quite frequently, which made him happy, but he knew that Lucas did too, which made him uncomfortable, since, as everyone knew, the princess and Lucas had been sweethearts for a brief period some years ago, when they had still been at their lessons. Indeed, it had generally been assumed then that she and Lord Lucas would one day wed, as they seemed an appropriate social match.

Juliana laughed at this now, she told Bostock, because their liaison had been mere adolescent experimentation, not serious. Personally, she saw no need to wed, and if she ever did, she assured Bostock, it would not be to her old friend Lucas, who was like a brother to her now.

Indeed, Bostock knew, Juliana's youth had not been overly prudish, nor even sheltered. Like many of the young women of her class in this liberal state, she had had much freedom and her share of experimentation. Bostock remembered the hot nights when he had stayed up late with his books with his casement windows open, knowing that Juliana and Lucas were out in a meadow, sleeping naked together in the dewy grass.

Bostock remembered this again, now, as he strolled with the princess one early summer day, in a steaming field, drowsy with poppies. He walked behind her, idly chopping at the long grass with a switch, and amusing her with court gossip. She wandered slowly, holding up the hem of her dress, towards the edge of the field where there was a tree and a stream. One strap of the dress had fallen, lazy with heat, to reveal a shoulder that shone slightly with perspiration.

"So Anton of course pretended not to be shocked," said Count Bostock, "but his eyes were wide as . . ." He paused, squinting up at the hazy sun. "As, as *casseroles*."

Ahead of him, the princess laughed.

"Really, he stiffened and smiled and toyed with his glass — such lovely glasses, Erika always serves in, at Elmflere, like glass seashells, they're from Syllyrica, I think, she imports them specially — but his eyes, truly, betrayed utter *terror*, my dear, like a cat, like the eyes of a cat who suddenly sees a strange face in a window. *Paralysed*. And what made it even more amusing was that I'm quite sure he didn't really even understand what she said, all he knew was that it was something *terribly* sinful and that he must appear not to be shocked."

"Poor old Anton," said the princess. "He wants so desperately to be dangerous. Here's the brook." She sat on the bank and took off her shoes.

The young count fell beside her, among the poppies and smell of earth by the water. He lay on his back and closed his eyes. The stream lapped quietly. He felt the heat of the day on him like a weight. His embroidered shirt stuck to his neck. He fanned himself with a cuff and said, "Like all young Lucas's friends, poor gentle beauties." He sighed. "So do we all, though, really. Want to be dangerous." He opened his eyes. "Although Anton really, he hasn't a clue how ridiculous he — have you heard how he's been slumming it? Oh yes. He takes Elisabeth into Stjornokh at night, in search of the *authentic*. Which always seems to mean simply seedy. *Loosh*, the Syllyricans would call it. They long for the *loosh*."

"The what?" said Juliana. She was chewing on a stem of grass, her chin on her knees, staring at the slow-moving water.

"At one with the common man, they are," said Bostock. "Fearlessly flouting social distinction. They even flirted with the whiskheads, for a time. One of the milder sects. I wonder what pleasures —"

"The what?" said the princess.

"The what what?"

"What did they flirt with, you said?"

"Whiskheads. In the capital. They attended some displays, but as I said, it was one of the milder sects, anyway —"

"What are whiskheads?"

Bostock sat up and looked at her. "Did you say what are whiskheads?"

"Yes." She was frowning.

"Whiskheads. Tangleheads. Mazebrains."

She shook her head.

"Oh my dear. I am so sorry. I had assumed everyone in my acquaintance was at least barely in the swim, and not in need of lessons in ancient history. Or recent fashion." He opened his mouth as if to explain, but frowned and lay down again. "They are of absolutely no importance. A passing trend."

"Oh come on. You can't do that. You can't just do that. Tell me."

"Tell you what?"

"*Bostock.* Tell me about the whiskheads. Who are they?"

He sighed again. "They don't call themselves mazebrains or whiskheads, of course. They give themselves quite noble names. Crafters, some of them pretentiously say. Convolutionists, though, seems to be the correct label among current adherents. Convolutionists." He looked at her anxiously. "I am not sure you will be entirely happy to hear all about them. But perhaps you should know."

"Go *on!*" she said, whipping her bare shin with her piece of grass.

Bostock looked momentarily at the exposed shin and bare feet in the sun, took a deep breath, and went on. "It is a trend among young people in the city, some of whom have made their homes — quite illegally, I might add — in the interior spaces of the Architectons. They practise a strange art. They like to . . . How shall I describe it? *Insert*, into their heads, through their ears and right through their brains —"

"*Insert?* Insert what?"

"Yes, not mutilate, for it is very carefully done so as not to damage the very fine filaments of metal, crafted by the ancient jewellers of the villages — and they have actually brought some of them into the city, where I'm sure they are most ill at ease —"

"Into their *brains?*"

"I am explaining," said Bostock, "if you will only *listen*. The skill consists in inserting the wire — they use silver, usually, or a copper-silver alloy, for fineness — in one ear, through the convolutions of the brain so as not to actually *pierce* the delicate membranes of the brain, winding the filament through the long and complex tunnels, so it actually emerges out the other ear."

"Is it not painful?"

"Extremely. The operation takes several hours, several hours of exquisite agony. The victim — willing victim, one assumes — must be strapped down so as not to tear the wires from the guiding hand. Only the most skilled crafters can perform it without killing the patient. Now, it appears, the whiskhead youth are themselves learning to perform the act."

"What about their ears, their eardrums?"

"The wires are so fine that the tiny perforation in the eardrum does not damage the hearing. In fact, some of them claim, the presence of the protruding wire, like an antenna, actually enhances their hearing. They claim they hear the beauty of the whistling wind even where there is none. A dubious pleasure."

"But . . ." Juliana whipped her piece of grass up and down. "Why would anyone want to do something so painful, deliberately?"

"Well." Bostock gestured vaguely. "They make all sorts of claims. Anyone who emerges from such a dangerous and painful procedure is understandably very proud. They feel they have emerged stronger from an ordeal. And they . . . well, they say their brains are altered. They speak of enhanced perception and wider consciousness and union of body and soul and so on and so on. They seem not to worry about the philosophical complexity of such a distinction in the first place, but at any rate, some of them, the most respected, have had several wires inserted. Then they have the ends of the wires, outside their heads, woven into fine patterns like jewellery. You can hardly see this of course, the wires are so fine, but in the right light you can identify them by the glitter around their ears, like a cloud of fireflies. It is most amusing. And of course by their odd clothes — they wear a strange mix of hard fabrics imported from our neighbour — a shiny oilskin sort of stuff made from the sap of a southern tree and refined in great factories — and peasant garb, like the leather trousers and wooden shoes of old men. The girls cut their hair short. They look abominable."

Juliana ran a hand through her thick hair and stared across the field. She shook her head to clear a drop of perspiration forming on her brow. "Who are they? What kind of child would do this?"

Bostock shrugged. "All kinds. They come from the slums of the capital — not that there are many," he said quickly, "but as you know there are the troublesome quarters, and of course some of them are educated, some the children of the wealthy, and some have come from the villages. They all . . ." He hesitated.

Juliana looked at him intently. "Why did you say I wouldn't want to know about them?"

"Well . . . because they are not pleasant. They are a rather angry sort. They have political meetings at which there is much shouting and jeering, they don't respect the local ordnances . . . they are unhappy."

"They are unhappy? About what?"

He looked away.

"About me," she said.

"Yes."

She was silent.

Gently, he said, "About everything, I think, but your name does come up. You represent . . ."

"Everything."

"Yes."

Juliana's face was red, her body rigid. She stood up. "Why has nobody informed me of this discontent?"

"Oh come, come, it is of extremely minor . . ."

She was putting on her shoes. "I must get back."

"Oh, Princess, please, please don't let a trivial slight disturb our peaceful afternoon. We have only just begun to relax. Look, the sun is still high, there are myriad pleasant —"

"Enjoy the sun. I'll get back on my own."

Bostock sighed. "I see I am to take the blame for the rudeness of the whiskheads."

She began to walk away.

He called after her, "In every state there will be mal-contents."

She stopped and turned to him. "Not in my king-dom. Not in Liralove."

He watched her stride away through the field, her red hair streaming behind her.

🖎 THAT NIGHT SHE WAS UNABLE to sleep. She lay in her cool chamber with the windows open. Faint sounds of horses' hoofs drifted up from the streets of the city below. She rose and walked through the archway to her private garden, a high-walled enclosure accessible only to her, and only through her bedroom.

This garden was further evidence of the ingenuity of Liralovian architects: high in the castle, in a tower that overhung the walls, it held earth and even a narrow rock pool for the princess to bathe in. Its walls were arched colonnades thick with vines, brushed by the leaves of exotic trees, in which squabbled imported birds of bright plumage and eerie cries. Her bathing pool was deep and dark with smooth rock sides, its water still as black glass, with petals floating on the slick surface of scented oil.

Juliana stood in the garden, breathing in the heavy smell of green. The calls of the orange bird rang in her head like the jeers and laughter of a whiskhead meeting. She shook herself to banish the image, and then felt a pang of regret as she thought of Bostock lying alone on

the riverbank in the sun. She sighed, unfastened her gown and let it drop to the floor. Naked, she walked through the shrubs to the rock pool; she piled and pinned her hair up before lowering herself into the water.

It was like sinking into cool velvet. She breathed deeply.

She had seen young people, on her visits to town, who dressed as Bostock had described, with short hair and shirts made of the strange new imported material that was shiny like oilskin but stretched like silk. In fact, she had seen it in her own palace: one of her maids had a pale daughter who lived with her in the servants' quarters off the central courtyard, who came and went and wore such things. Juliana had taken an interest in the girl and given her her own castoffs.

Juliana considered. She already had an old pair of suspendered peasant shorts, buried in a dress-up trunk. All she needed would be the more modern element. She would have to ask her maid, as early as she could wake her in the morning, to discreetly borrow some things for her. It would be easy to invent a costume party. Faithful Gally would love to play along.

The princess hauled herself out of the bath and made for her bed. For now, she had a plan.

A HALF-HOUR AFTER THE sun rose she already had the sleepy Gally rifling her daughter's drawer. In the princess's chamber the older woman chuckled as Juliana wriggled into a borrowed tunic. The princess was surprised by the sticky feel of the fabric, the tenacity of its grip on skin. She looked at herself in the mirror and felt hard and sleek. Over the tunic she buckled the peasant shorts, and over her legs she pulled woollen tights. Then she stepped into a pair of peasant's clogs.

She thanked the giggling Gally and sent her back to bed. Alone, the princess studied her gangly appearance and frowned. She tried piling her hair into its bun again, but that made her look even softer. She spent a moment leaning on her windowsill, hearing the city come to life below. Then, trying to breathe slowly, she turned to a drawer and pulled out a pair of gardening shears. She sat at her dressing table for a long moment, staring at her reflection, the shears in her lap.

Then, with trembling hands, she lifted the cutters and grasped a handful of thick red hair. She closed her eyes and clipped.

She felt the lock slip down her leg. She could not open her eyes. She could almost hear the tangle hit the floor; *whoomp*, the sound of a sigh.

When she opened her eyes they were full of tears. She saw the gap in her red mane like a wound, and after that it was easier. With tears coursing on her cheeks, she cropped her entire head, the tresses falling about.

She finished the rough coiffure with nail scissors. She giggled with the giddiness that comes after tears, appalled, as she realized how small was her skull. She looked like a furry forest creature, perhaps some kind of rodent — much like the schoolgirls she had seen loitering in city squares.

Still she frowned. Something was missing. No matter how she grimaced and scowled, her face looked delicate, privileged, soft. Naked. She opened a wooden box on her dressing table and took out the brushes and pots she had not used since adolescence. With wide eyes, she painted her face: grape-purple lips, raccoon eyes, pallid corpse skin, a sombre glow on the cheekbones.

She gnashed her teeth at the mirror. This was good. This would pass.

She slipped through the dim corridors of the palace, down back stairways towards the servants' wing. Without the bleary bakers noticing her, she passed through hot kitchens, and then she was through the smallest gate in the rear wall. The day was warm and clear. She followed the castle walls until she came to the main gate. Feeling dwarfed by the palace walls, tiny in her heavy clogs, she began her walk down the steep and dusty road to Stjornokh. She heard the massive town bell chime below, nine times.

 **HE CITY NO LONGER BEGAN AT THE STURDY STONE** gates; it had swelled and drifted into the surrounding plain. Houses, gardens, shops of dull brick. There were hardly any stone houses to be seen; most were made of wooden planks and thatch. Just outside the gates Juliana passed a sprawling building surrounded by grassless ground. The brick was yellow, cut with rows of small oblong windows. She paused and walked towards it, only to recoil as she saw the inscription carved in stone above the doorway: Princess Juliana Grammar School of Outer Stjornokh.

She felt herself blush as she became angry. She could not recall opening this school, or even being consulted about the use of her name. She had never even approved the plans. She had no idea who was responsible. It was an outrage. Of course, it would not have offended her so much had the school not been so hideous, so spectacularly hideous. She considered. In fact, its hideousness lay in its being so fanatically *un*spectacular, in being so deeply and entirely inoffensive. She kicked at a stone, determined that on returning to the castle she would find the name of the architect responsible, and the school board who had used her name. And she continued on her way.

Soon she was in the city proper, in the narrow residential streets where every window bore a flower box full of bright petals and the walls rustled with vines. She smiled, just as awed by the houses' great height as she had been as a child: to her, the word *house* meant a low stone one with a wall and a garden, like the peasants' cottages dotting the woods where she had played. And when, on special occasions, she was dressed up and admonished to be good and taken into the city in a carriage, she had stared up at the tiny dormer windows poking out of slate roofs, many some four or even *five* storeys up, so high you became dizzy with looking — not nearly as high as her own palace, of course, but that was a palace, and these were houses — and she had imagined the cosy apartments under the roofs and thought of her own palace and the wonder of men's structures.

She looked up now at the same facades leaning against one another as if jostling for space, with stones, beams, and plaster arched in crazy patterns all the way up to the little dormer windows in the same slate roofs, and smiled.

She was approaching a market square: she heard the shouting and smelled freshly baked bread. It made her stomach groan for breakfast. She wrinkled her nose: there was another smell in the air, under the warmth, a bad one, like swamp water. As she followed the cobblestones of the winding streets towards the market, the odour seemed to grow stronger, and soon she recognized it as that of sewage. So Lucas had a point.

Indeed, in some of the gutters dribbled a dark sludge she preferred not to look at. She would try to talk to Lucas about his bill as soon as possible.

As she came out of shadow into the light of the market square, she gasped: the market stalls were grouped around the base of a famous Architecton, one of the smaller ones, a lumpy affair of large coloured blocks and solid triangles, from which soared a delicate needle of a tower, ringed with steel platforms. It reared high above them, glowing a strange pale grey in the morning light.

While Juliana was studying the tower, a notice pasted to the wall next to her caught her eye: "Notice to All Right-minded Citizens." And so she moved closer to read it.

It was a call to a demonstration against "non-practical architecture," signed by one T. Kornmuse — a name she recognized; a friendly, smiling city councillor she had met at boring meetings. The notice warned that the social fabric of the city was degenerating and public morality eroding, that youths with no values or respect for their elders were partly responsible, that these same youths and no one else benefitted from the vast and sinful sums spent by decadent citizens on shamelessly non-practical architecture, wasteful indulgences that were inevitably eyesores.

The princess was a full two paragraphs into this strange text before she realized that it was about the Architectons. She scowled and read on.

The tract warned that the wasteful architecture was becoming home to many delinquents, seething hotbeds of bad practices such as keeping late hours, drinking, rudeness, and who knew what else. It called for destruction of the ugliest towers and an end to all such spending — since all money would be better put to use in building much-needed schools, healthy gymnasiums, and a more sanitary sewage system. The demonstration was scheduled for that very morning — ten o'clock, in the central square.

On finishing the notice, Juliana laughed rudely herself, and she didn't care who saw her. She would have to find out more about T. Kornmuse on her return. In the meantime, she needed breakfast.

She walked through the shouting men, the women in long, old-fashioned dresses, and the scents of grilled pond eel and runny cheese and fresh flowers, and bought herself a warm bun and a mug of hot herb-water. She kept her eyes down as she spoke to the merchant at his stall, nervous that she would be recognized, but he hardly glanced at her. People strode around her as if she were invisible.

She leaned against the base of the Architecton and sipped her tea. She saw that the plaster was badly cracked, the stone scratched and scribbled on, strange painted inscriptions she didn't understand. There were several young people sitting or standing near her, three girls and two boys, dressed as she was, laughing and pushing one another. Two of the girls has spiky hair like hers, but one had long brown hair in pigtails.

With a pang, Juliana ran her hand over her own furry scalp. She stared covertly. She could make out no signs of wires coming from their heads.

As she wandered away, she wondered where those girls lived, why they weren't in school or working in fields or in shops, as she had been told everyone did. There were many things she didn't understand.

As she made her way towards the central square, she noticed that the houses lining the narrow streets were less well kept: instead of flower boxes, laundry hung on every windowsill. She began to pass beggars and thin children who watched from doorways. The streets grew narrower and twistier, the sewage smells worsened, until she no longer knew in which direction she moved. A group of young men in heavy clogs brushed against her as they passed, laughing, and she began to be frightened, thinking she was lost.

But she turned a corner and stepped into light again, and looked up at the greatest Architecton of all, the tall towers of emerald stone and useless staircases she could see from her palace window. She sighed in amazement. It seemed to pierce the very sky.

This was the central square, a wide open space with noble facades all around it, the meeting point of many streets. But she saw that the facades were dilapidated now, the shops boarded up, and today there was much shouting. The demonstration had begun: a crowd of people carrying placards was clustered about the base of the Architecton. A man was on a platform, shouting. She moved into the crowd and recognized Councillor Kornmuse, red-faced and waving his fist. But what she noticed first was the garbage under her feet: loose paving stones, broken glass, paper.

"And what," Councillor Kornmuse was shouting, "would our beloved ruler, our pure and lovely princess, think of this excess and pretension, this waste, this *abomination!*" The crowd roared and waved their signs. "She who has nothing but noble taste and innocent practices, what would she think? And would she not be ashamed —" he paused, "a-*shamed* of this squalor, these *costumes?*"

He gestured behind him, and Juliana could see, through the crowd, that there was a smaller crowd beyond him. Hunched in the shadow of the Architecton, youths in worn clothing sat silently, arms folded.

Juliana looked around. Most of the protestors seemed to be of middle age, and wore clean and conservative clothing. She noticed one woman with a hard face staring at her. Juliana smiled politely. The woman waggled a finger at her and grimaced. "No shame," she snarled. "None of you. No shame."

Juliana stepped back in surprise, then remembered her hair, her makeup, the viscous blouse. She averted her eyes.

But the woman had stepped close to her, was tugging at her shiny sleeve. "Go and join your friends," she rasped. "Go on, go and join them. But I" — She waggled her finger again, frowning fearfully— "I feel for your mother. I feel for her. And —" She raised her finger skyward.

Juliana stared at her, fascinated. The woman's face was contorted with anger or something like it; fear, perhaps. Her thin fingers gripped the princess's arm.

"For our princess, our noble princess. Think of her. Just think of her." The woman released her painful grip, and Juliana pushed her way through the crowd.

As she crossed the small open space between the demonstrators and the youths, the crowd jeered and whistled. "Hussy!" one man yelled. "Prodigal!" shouted a woman. Juliana's face stung, as if someone had slapped her. No one had ever shouted at her before.

The boys around the base of the Architecton hardly looked up as she approached. The archways opening on the structure's great inner hollows were boarded up, the boards scrawled with graffiti. There had once been glass panes in the spaces and skylights on the first two levels, but most were now broken, some covered with paper.

Clearly, the square arch that sheltered most of the youth from the sun served as an entrance to the great dark structure; a doorway was cut in the boards, and young men came and went from the shadows, leaning against the massive stone buttresses, clapping each other on the back, puffing on weed pipes. Juliana stepped between them; a young woman with hair shaved in strips smiled at her, and Juliana smiled back.

She went through the rough doorway in the arch, stepping over boards that were knee-high, and found she was in a high-ceilinged tunnel leading to a bright open space. The walls were papered with notices, some bearing announcements, some drawings and poems. She emerged into a spectacular atrium, its sloping walls made of coloured glass, which came to a point many storeys above. One side of the atrium was in fact the outer wall of the central tower; through the glass she could see it, looming over them.

There was a smell of spices and hot oil in the air, and a low murmur of conversation: all over the cracked paving stones of the atrium, youths in canvas and leather sat and talked in the blue-green light. They wore both the fine slippers of the merchant class and the heavy clogs of the peasant, but those who wore leather slippers had worn them down or painted them in fine patterns, and wore them with no laces. Some youths were heating herb-water and frying cakes on little oil stoves; many had sleeping rolls with them. They all seemed to be quite calm, ignoring the demonstration outside, talking and smoking in the odd, filtered light.

The princess looked up. Suspended by ropes and braces, precarious stairways and ladders ran up the sides

of the pyramid, leading to platforms, openings, and more corridors. The place must be vast. The ladders and scaffolding seemed built of scavenged material; they had obviously been pieced together by the building's new inhabitants. On some platforms, newly built shelters, made with sheets and boards, seemed to perch on the walls like birds' nests.

Juliana wandered across the atrium and into another tunnel; this one sloped gently upwards, and soon she was on another level, also crowded with young men and women, and the little cubicles they had made with sheets of cheap wood and metal, to create a little privacy in which to sleep.

Juliana peeped over one partition as she passed and glimpsed a girl with pigtails and a long-haired boy lying sleeping together in a blanket; the girl's chest was bare and the boy's hand lay gently on her little breast. Their pale skins were exactly the same colour, their hair the same length; without the swellings of new breasts and the nipples like buds, one could not have told them apart.

Suddenly the girl opened her eyes and caught Juliana's gaze. Juliana blushed red and moved on, keeping her eyes on the floor.

She moved ever upwards through the labyrinthine structure. She passed rooms whose doorways were hung with gauzy curtains of embroidered cloth. Musky scents and faint candlelight emanated from these rooms; she did not dare to look in. She passed sudden vast squares of light, windows ten feet tall which looked over the maze of grey streets below. She passed walls painted with murals, strange images which seemed to tell mythological tales, sketchy architectural drawings, and everywhere slogans and symbols.

Some of the slogans hurt her. She saw one that said, "Take the princess for a walk"; below it was scrawled, "The princess does not live; the palace is a mausoleum."

She saw fantastical clothing and much fine traditional jewellery — she even saw an old peasant with a full white beard and a leather suitcase which, she knew, carried metalworking tools — but no one with a mutilated head. She began to think the whiskheads were a myth. Bostock was known to exaggerate.

She had no idea where in the structure she was, or how high she had climbed, when she came to a little café in a bulge in the wall: it had a bar like a merchant's stall, and behind it a row of ceramic jugs, a stove and a cast-iron tureen of hot soup, and three little bar stools. Red light came from a stained-glass panel in the wall. Behind the bar was a doorway covered with a cloth, and a boy with a wild beard and studs in his nose and lip. He folded his arms and frowned slightly as she sat down.

She smiled to mask her nervousness and looked through the red window. She gasped as she saw how high up she was. There was nothing below her but space, and a grid of streets and church steeples.

The bartender grunted. She looked at him and said,

"Ah, hello. What do you have to drink?"

He shrugged and growled, "Kaash."

"I'm sorry?"

"Only kaash." He sighed as if frustrated and pointed to the jugs, and at a little slate with words on it in chalk. It read: "Glass, Half-jug, Full Jug," with three prices.

The princess knew she was appearing ignorant, and the prices all seemed very cheap, so she cleared her throat and said, "A half-jug, please."

The bartender raised his eyebrows slightly and reached behind him for a jug and a dark glass mug. He poured a thick black liquid and set it before her.

She thanked him and paid, and gingerly brought the heavy glass to her nose. As she smelled it, her head spun with the smell of earth and musk and she knew what it was; she had tasted it in the country, while opening a fair, an agricultural show. She peered at the muddy liquid; it was dark purple, not black. So this was what they called the wine now, Kaash.

She tasted and remembered the rich and bitter aroma of quine, the country flower whose purple petals were wrapped so tightly they made a sort of flesh, like a fruit. The peasants drank a wine made of fermented quine petals. It even tasted purple, velvet and earthy, or mineral. It was an ancient drink.

She knew the bartender was watching from the corner of his eye so she drank deeply.

It was like drinking melted quartz.

The bartender was ignoring her now, flexing his fore-arms and looking absently at the people passing. She saw that his forearms were embroidered with fine wires — but she looked at his ears, and they appeared perfectly normal.

She sighed and turned to the notices and posters that clung to the wall. Her gaze was arrested by a small handbill with a complicated border, and the phrase "Brethren of Crafters."

She looked closely: "Convolutionists' evening: philos-ophy, music, performance, kaash." It gave today's date and the time — "eleven of the clock" — but gave no place.

Her heart beat faster, and she sipped her kaash. It was already making her warm. She said to the bartender, as casually as she could, "Are you going to the Convolutionists' evening tonight?"

He looked at her sharply and snorted as if she had said something funny.

She shrugged and said, "Well, I think I'll go."

"You will?"

She nodded.

"Uh-huh."

She sipped her kaash, hoping her face would not redden. He was staring at her, looking at her thin arms and neck.

"Well," he said finally. "Do you know where it is?"

"Well . . . not this one. I mean not this time. I've been to them before, of course, but . . ."

He was smiling a little. Now she began to blush.

"You sure you'd like to go?" he said gently.

She looked down at the bar and nodded. Then she looked up, her face on fire, and said, "Yes. Yes, I would."

He looked at her. She held his gaze.

He paused a long moment and said, "Just a minute," and disappeared behind the curtain.

He murmured to someone, and another man appeared, an older one. He looked disgruntled, as if he had been disturbed. He too frowned and folded his arms. He was bigger and stronger than the bartender but had the same sparkle of wire on his forearms. The bartender appeared behind him and whispered something in his ear. The older man nodded and stroked his thin goatee, staring at Juliana as if appraising her.

As his head moved, Juliana's heart thudded. There was a distinct metallic flash to the right of his head. He leaned towards her, into the light, and she saw, for a second, the fine net of wires that protruded from each ear. The light danced around his head; the wires seemed to whirr. Her mouth nearly fell open.

He looked her up and down and moved out of the light so his wires disappeared again, except for disjointed glints like fireflies. He looked back at the bartender, who shrugged, and he smiled. "All right," he said in a gentle voice. "Sapphire quadrant. Level seven. Eleven o'clock." He backed into the shadow. "Amuse yourself." And he was gone.

Juliana breathed deeply. Her heart was beating wildly. "Thank you," she said.

When she left the bar she felt warm and drowsy. She wandered to another glassed atrium, which had several ceilings of coloured glass and swaying platforms overhead made of little but metal grids. She found another food counter and ordered a bowl of soup. A smiling bartender with a bald head explained that the odd symbols she had seen on the walls denoted quadrant and level; they were in emerald quadrant now. He made her memorize the staircases and passages to sapphire seven, and smiled when she repeated them correctly.

She ordered another half-jug of ancient quine wine, and passed the rest of the afternoon gazing upwards at the shards of coloured glass, entranced by the shifting ceilings, the moving light, the spinning platforms of wire mesh.

THREE

T WAS
NOT REALLY
DESIGNED AS
A ROOM, THE
Convolutionists'   meeting
hall; nothing inside the
Architecton had been, of course. All these interiors had
been left unconstructed, just spaces on a plan, an architect's experiment with "visual silences" and falling patterns of light. The hall was a mere hollow, the interior
of a great plaster cube stuck to the outside of the
tower. It was entered through trap doors cut in its
floor; there were no windows. The residents had built a
stage at one end and a bar at the other, and hung the
walls with candles, bowls of burning herbs, and
embroidered fabrics.

It was midnight and still the spectacle had not
begun. Juliana leant against the bar and narrowed her eyes
in the smoke, searching the crowd for glinting jewellery.
There were many bracelets and earrings, many boys with

painted faces and girls in boys' clothes, but no pierced heads. No whiskheads.

Juliana clutched her mug of kaash. She felt a little better than she had when awakened that evening by darkness and lamp-lighting, her head on her numb forearms, on the bar counter. She had felt refreshed by the sleep, and had eaten some more, but the afternoon of kaash had left her distanced, contemplative. And here she was drinking it again. The smoke around her seemed warm; the candlelight a fuzzy glow.

The room was really crowded now, and there was a new buzz in the air. She fixed on a tall blond boy alone against the stage. He wore a loose cotton peasant's shirt. His eyes swept the room as if searching for someone. As he moved his head, she noticed the glint near his ears, and she sat up straight. He was smiling at someone now, greeting a friend, and the ends of his many wire inserts flashed and danced like a halo.

Juliana watched him shake hands firmly with other boys, and kiss a lovely girl with long red hair. Juliana felt a pain as she saw them talk, and she ran her hand again over her own scalp. The girl's hair flashed too; she had several inserts.

The small group of whiskheads seemed so confident: they spoke easily, languourously, always touching each other a little — a hand on a shoulder or fingering a lock of hair. They laughed frequently, and waved their weed pipes about just as her uncle Osbert used to do, as if it were a joke in itself. In fact, watching them she was generally reminded of her father's friends smoking pipes in the library — of Lady Patricia, who played the gabbler, the traditional stringed instrument like a bulbous guitar, of uncle Osbert, the great architect who had designed one of the smaller Architectons and built it with his own money . . .

Juliana sighed, envious. She turned to the bar and ordered another glass of kaash. There was a new bartender now, a whiskhead too. There were suddenly whiskheads all around her, laughing roughly and slapping each other, boys and girls. She felt a little dizzy and held onto the bar.

She saw two odd-looking people emerging through the trap door entrance, and their clothes weren't quite right: the young man's hair was sleek and combed, the young woman wore a long cotton dress such as one might see in a respectable part of town. Juliana started as she realized that she recognized their faces: Count Anton and his cousin Elisabeth. They were looking around, smiling nervously.

Juliana cursed to herself and turned away, keeping her face turned down towards the bar. She took a gulp of kaash. She looked across the room in the other direction and saw the tall blond boy, looking at her. He smiled, and before she could think about it, she smiled back. She cursed herself again and turned to face the wall. It seemed there was nowhere she could look.

"Ladies, gentlemen, brethren of Convolutionists!" someone was roaring. The buzz subsided as all turned to face the stage. Careful not to present her full face in the direction of Anton and Elisabeth, the princess slowly turned to watch.

The first event was a series of readings by agitated whiskhead boys, long essays in rhyming couplets, denouncing the uncaring aristocracy. Juliana listened closely but soon lost interest: the poems were carefully made, with the occasional clever rhyme, but not nearly as amusing as they could have been. Count Bostock would have done it more delicately and viciously, she judged.

Cautiously, she cast a glance in the direction of her two acquaintances from court, only to see them disappearing down the trap door. Past their bedtime, she imagined.

After the poems there were musicians, apparently young peasants, playing folk tunes on traditional instruments: a lovely old gabbler, a wind-driven holtor, which was like an organ, and a ceramic furlpipe, which was like a flute.

The music was soft and lilting, and the crowd grew quiet. It was the simplest and saddest of tunes. Juliana was still, awash in nostalgia for the country. She wondered if the whiskheads knew that this was her father's favourite music, that he played the holtor himself alone in his study. Bostock had certainly said nothing about the whiskheads' love of these tunes. Probably he had not known.

She glanced at the blond boy again. He was standing rigid by the stage, listening closely. She watched his friends swaying slightly, still keeping their hands in the lightest contact with each other, as if passing a current between them.

After the music there was loud applause. The master of ceremonies announced, "Prepare for the wire music!" and there was even more applause.

Then three half-naked men wheeled in an amazingly complicated machine. Juliana's eyes opened wide as she saw both men and machine: the men had shaved heads and hairless bodies, and wore nothing but silk loincloths which covered their genitals and passed between their buttocks. They must have shaved their chests and legs to make their muscles gleam so — all inlaid with shining patterns of fine wires, from their calfs to their taut chests, making half-submerged images of peacocks, phalluses, and architectural drawings, which shifted and rippled as they laboured with the heavy machine. Around their heads glittered the signs of multiple insertions. Juliana gulped as she imagined the hours of voluntary agony and danger each man must have endured.

But the machine was even more intricate, all cogs and cranks and levers, and rows of glass tubes and metal blades. Juliana could not imagine its function.

Each man seized one of the protruding crank handles and began to turn slowly. The crowd was again quiet, and for a few seconds there was total silence.

The machine produced a grating sound, like metal grinding metal. It became regular, a sort of a beat, although it was difficult to follow. Over the grating began a high and ethereal wailing, like the sound of a fine wine-glass being stroked. It grew to be a siren, then began subtly changing pitch.

As the men cranked faster, layers of noise were added: thumps and bleats and shudders, and more glass-like wails. They began to form a tune, a mournful song like that made by wind in caves.

Juliana found herself swaying as she listened; people were beginning to dance, slowly and sensually, alone.

The beat quickened, and the tune grew more clear, and the noises ever more aggressive, until the machine sounded like a whole orchestra of machines, producing an inhuman symphony which was both titillating and jangling. It was unmistakably the noise of a factory, yet still beautiful.

Juliana felt sad and stimulated and troubled. Perhaps it was the kaash: the images swayed around her. Then, without knowing how she got there, she was in the middle of the dancing crowd by the stage, whirling. The air was thick with heads and arms, herb-smoke and kaash and wailing. A couple near her kissed each other as they danced. The princess was breathing fast; the music was so harsh and yet so pretty it brought tears to her eyes.

It was from this point that Juliana had trouble, later, remembering with exact detail.

She found she was dancing close to the tall blond boy, that his face was pretty as a girl's, that his arms were around her and she was resting her head on his breast as they moved together. She parted his rough shirt at the neck and ran her fingers over his smooth chest, feeling the metallic edges of wires under the skin, the faint bristles of their ends. She breathed in his scent.

And then she was following him through dark passages and up ladders, holding onto his hand, and then she was in a candlelit room with a glass floor, hung with gauzy sheets, high above the city's towers. She fell onto a mattress covered with rumpled silk and tried to think. The blond boy leaned against a big wooden chest.

The room seemed to be a sort of bubble stuck to the side of the tower; if she looked over the side of the sprawling bed she grew dizzy. The gauzy hangings fluttered in a breeze from somewhere, and fresh flowers were strewn on the glass floor. Herbs burned, and the mattress was deep and soft.

She sat up and shook her head. "This is your room?"

"My own." The boy was pulling off his shirt. His voice was as deep and soft as the bed.

"It is like flying, like being borne by a white bird." She stood and approached him. The ends of the wires hovering about his ears quivered. She reached a hand towards them, and he flinched. "I may not touch?"

"Carefully. They're delicate."

"What does it do to you if I touch? Is it painful?"

"There is some pain. But a light touch from a woman such as you can bring . . ."

"What?"

"Something I can't describe."

"Is it sound?"

"It is partly sound. A constant music in my head, which comes from movement, presences. Like yours. They are sensitive. But the music is feeling, it is something I feel. I can't describe it. It is like pain but not. It is like . . ." He shrugged. "I told you I couldn't explain."

As lightly as she could, she blew on the filaments by his right ear. He trembled and groaned a little. When he stopped quivering, he was breathing fast. "It is as if," he said, "as if you were breathing on me from inside. Breathing on my brain. I feel your warm breath in my spine, in my . . . I don't know."

"I'm jealous," she said. "I wish I could know what it felt like."

"There is a way," he murmured. He bent to kiss her neck.

She backed against the chest. "No." He pushed himself against her. She placed her palms against his smooth chest. "Listen," she said.

"I'm listening." He took her face in his hands and kissed her mouth.

Juliana's head sang. His heart beat under her palms. The ends of his wires were dancing before her eyes, and she could swear — no, she was sure she heard a whirring as they moved, like tiny whipcords cutting the air. It was like a singing that she could only hear when his lips were close to hers. He was kissing her neck, pulling down the straps of the peasant overalls, inching up the tight blouse.

"Listen, I'm . . ." She stopped, shuddering, as the blouse moved up over her breasts; her arms lifted over her head as if of their own accord, and he pulled the top off entirely. She closed her eyes.

She felt her nipples swell and harden in the air, and then his lips on them, gently kissing. It occurred to her again, distantly, that this was a very bad idea, even an extremely bad idea. She tried to remind herself that she was a princess, the ruler of a sovereign nation, on a mission which was political and social and practical in intent.

He took a nipple between his lips; she felt the faint edge of teeth and the warmth spreading between her legs. She was breathing rapidly. If she didn't stop now, it would certainly be too late.

She opened her eyes. Over the top of his blond head, the room came into focus, its dim oil lamp and gauzy hangings. She shook her head. "No," she gasped.

He did not stop.

"No," she said clearly. And pushed him gently away.

He lifted his head and looked her quizzically in the eyes.

"I'm sorry." She cast around her for her shirt, her heart pounding. "I'm sorry, I can't. I can't go on."

The boy narrowed his eyes and smiled. He took a step back.

"Look," she said, picking up the blouse. "I . . . there's something you don't understand. I would love to explain but I can't. I can't be here, and I can't explain why."

The boy shrugged, smiling grimly, and sat down on the low bed. He picked up his pipe and lit it, watching her as she dressed. When she turned to face him he was lying back, smoking.

"Look," she said, "you mustn't think I just . . ."

He shrugged. "Yes. I understand. I thought so. I had a feeling you weren't —"

"I wasn't what?"

The boy hesitated. "You're not from here. I can tell by your voice. Where are you from? From around the market square, where the merchants live? Or from outer Stjornokh?"

"What does it matter?" she said, irritated. She felt quite sober now, and her mouth was dry.

He shrugged scornfully. "I half expected this. I knew you weren't . . . for real."

She blushed hotly now and looked down. "No, no, I wish . . ." She shook her head. "Never mind. I'm sorry. I must go."

He nodded, but did not rise.

She was about to move through the curtained doorway when she paused and said, "How do I get out?"

"You are in ruby nine," he said with exaggerated politeness. "Take the first ladder on the left, then keep right and follow the symbols. It is not dangerous, miss."

She sighed. In the doorway, her hand on the curtain, she stopped short again. Softly, looking at the floor, she murmured, "What is your name?"

"My name? Jan. Jan is my name."

Before he could ask her anything, she was gone.

⤜ BY THE TIME SHE HAD trudged through the empty streets and all the way up the long hill to the castle, a grey light was bathing the hills. Soon the palace kitchens would be bustling; making an entrance would not be easy.

She tried the small door at the base of one of the rear towers and it opened easily; she was thankful that security had never been a worry for the royal family of Liralove. So she slipped again through the crepuscular servants' corridors and up narrow staircases and arrived unnoticed at her own tower. Her head throbbed, her legs ached from walking, and her feet bled from the chafing of the heavy clogs.

Clogs in hand, she tiptoed down the dark passage that led to her apartment, but a few metres from her door she stopped in fright: a dark form waited in shadow outside her door; a man in a black cape. She sank into a hollow in the wall, then cautiously poked her head out to peer at him.

The man shifted and turned to look in her direction; in the darkness she could not see his face. She held her breath. She could either stand as silently as she could or turn and run.

The man moved again, and her heart thudded. She was about to make her dash when his voice rang out, an old man's voice: "Juliana?"

She sighed and relaxed and stepped into the light of an embrasure. "Yes, Father," she said. "It's me."

King Harvor shuffled to meet her. As he came into the light, she saw that he looked exhausted as well; he wore pyjamas under his cape.

"Father!" she said. "Have you been waiting for me all . . ." She trailed off as she saw the look of horror on his face. He was staring with an open mouth at her haircut, her makeup, her odd costume.

"Father," she said quickly, "don't be upset, it's not what you —"

"Juliana!" he moaned, "not you too! Not like one of those *wastrels*. Surely you haven't —"

"No, Father, no, I can explain every —" She paused. "Father, what, may I ask, are you doing skulking outside my chamber door, in the darkness?"

The old man looked at the floor. "I was worried," he mumbled. "Just wanted to make sure you were . . . you were . . ."

"Well. I am. I am whatever you want. I am fine, Father. I don't want you to worry about me. I . . ."

He was looking away. He seemed immensely sad. "I truly thought *you*, you would be the last to . . . the last to . . ."

She took his hand. "Father, it was sweet of you to worry about me. And I am sorry to upset you, but it's not . . . it's nothing to worry about. I can't . . . really. Nothing to worry about."

He nodded, looking old.

"Father, I am very, very tired. Good night."

He nodded again and shuffled down the passage, his head bowed.

Juliana sighed and entered her chamber. The moment she fell onto her bed, she was asleep.

FOUR

H E WOKE EARLY IN THE AFTERNOON, BATHED, AND immediately began summoning advisors to the throne room. They all gaped at her cropped head, but she gave them their orders so briskly they dared not comment. "Lord Armstreme, Minister of the Interior, I want a written report of the activities of City Councillor Kornmuse of Stjornokh. Officer Bude, I want your men to bring me all the information they have on the sect of the Convolutionists, sometimes known as Crafters, commonly known as whiskheads — their origins, habits, dwellings, beliefs, everything. I want all this as soon as possible, tomorrow if you can. Officer Kantor —"

"Your highness," interrupted Bude with a cough.

The princess looked at him impatiently. She had always found Bude amusing, with his bald head and pudgy face, his meticulous application of rules. Bude never seemed to leave the palace, yet he was full of well-informed disapproval for the latest proposals; he shuffled about, worrying quietly to himself, ever ready with a patriotic maxim and a dire prediction. Now, his mouth pursed, his eyes gleaming in his puffy face, he looked like a chess player who has noticed an exposed bishop: he looked sly. "If Your Highness," he said in his high voice, "will permit me to make a suggestion."

"Yes, Officer Bude."

"It would be quite simple to provide, to establish rather, an effective, shall we say, *pipeline,* to the, say, *internal* proceedings of the so-called Convolutionists' group."

"I'm not sure I follow you."

Bude coughed again. "It would be quite simple, Your Highness, to place or *insert* an appropriately disguised and well-versed agent of the court — youthful appearance would, of course, be critical to his or indeed her ultimate acceptance by the groups, as indeed would be a careful study of the current argot or dialect thereof —"

"Insert where, Officer Bude?"

"As a source of accurate information, Your Highness, an agent of ours freely circulating among the very practitioners themselves would surely be most valuable?"

The princess frowned. "Do you mean a spy?"

He bowed stiffly. "An *accurate source* would perhaps be a more judicious appellation."

"You are proposing an informer."

"For the greater good of the populace, Your Highness, who are no doubt frightened by the most visible antisocial behaviour of these elements. A less biased source of much-needed information can scarcely be imagined."

Princess Juliana stood up. "Officer Bude. I regret to hear you proposing the use of spies in this domain. We will have no spying on citizens of this kingdom. Is that clear?"

He bowed again. "As Your Highness wishes."

Juliana sat again, and turned her head to the documents that needed her seal, hoping that no one would notice her blushing. She was blushing from guilt. She did not know how she could afford to be so pious with Bude on the subject of spying. Of course, she had been a spy herself. But she knew that Bude's idea of spying, and of what to do with the results of spying, would be different from hers.

⇚ OF ALL THE INTERVIEWS, documents, and drawings to which the princess attended over the next few days, it was perhaps her discussion with the great architect that troubled her most. She had reviewed much whiskhead art, some fine and some clumsy; she had read the scurrilous speeches, the vicious attacks on her government, her person — some of which obscurely mingled political resentment and sexual fantasy in a convoluted, frankly indecent, and rather frightening manner — and she was confused. The whiskheads seemed to love everything she loved, and yet they despised her. And when the perceptibly contemptuous Bude brought the famous architect to her presence, she was a little afraid.

His name was Crivello, and he looked, as Count Bostock would have put it, a trifle neglected. He wore no scarf to keep his collar closed, and his hair was wild. He was myopic, and peered through a pince-nez which dug red ruts in his nose. Ushered into the princess's presence, he sat abruptly, before being so invited, folded his arms, and glanced about him nervously as if distracted or displeased or late for a pressing appointment.

"Master Crivello," said Juliana, "thank you so much for agreeing to share your great sensitivity and expertise with those of us who would know more about your craft."

He grunted.

Juliana paused for a moment, collecting herself, and went on. She explained to him that she was interested in the artistic values of the whiskheads, and wished to know why they resented the traditions of the kingdom. She was adding that she much admired the bizarre Architecton he had designed, when Crivello stood up. He paced to the window and stood there, his hands clasped behind his back, staring out at the gleaming towers beneath them. Juliana was trying to formulate some subtle way of reminding him that to turn one's back on the monarch in private audience was rather more than a minor gaffe, when he spoke. "It is tradition they most desire," he said gruffly.

"Yes," she said. "I understand their interest in the great crafts of Liralove, many of which are sadly . . . on the wane. But I admire those crafts as well, why, I grew up with them, with beautiful things —"

"They don't know this," said Crivello, turning to face her. "They have no idea of the beauty of the inside of this palace."

"Well, no."

"Well, no. All they know of the palace is that it emanates tasteless officials who build ugly schools and tell them to behave themselves."

"But the palace — *we* are the ones who commissioned most of the Architectons. At least, my family was, not the government officially. Why, my uncle Osbert was largely responsible for funding the very building which brought you so much fame, and are you not greatly admired by the whiskheads?"

Crivello bowed slightly. "I am much indebted to your family. Your uncle, his grace Lord Osbert, is a man of much artistic sensitivity. But the distinction which you make between the government and your family is lost on the young brethren of Crafters."

"But of course there is a distinction. Of course Lord Osbert would not spend public money on his personal projects. That would be irresponsible. We don't do that — in a spirit of fair-mindedness."

Crivello shrugged. "The distinction is immaterial to me personally. Gold is gold, it makes buildings. But yes, the vast majority of the population of the city would indeed object very strongly if the palace spent large amounts of public money on further Architectons. They see them, as you know, as irresponsible. They would prefer —"

"Better sewage. I know."

"You see, Your Highness, the whiskheads, as they are known, would be greatly surprised to see this finely wrought tapestry hanging here in the throne room, or —" He raised his eyebrows suddenly. "That wire grille over the far embrasure. Do you mind if I take a closer look?"

"By all means."

Crivello strode to the window, where he remained for some moments peering at the grille through his pince-nez, his hands clasped behind his back. "Very fine," he said at length. "From Syllyrica?"

"Yes. My father thinks it is some three hundred years old."

"Hmmm. That sounds a bit old to me. Some of the connecting work could be by Jasten, or one of his sons. Two hundred, perhaps. Very rare, at any rate. Very fine." He traced the filigree with a delicate finger. "A great pleasure." He turned back to her and began to pace the chamber. "At any rate, the young brethren would be much surprised to see it here. They associate you with the glorious aesthetic of Councillor Kornmuse." He spat out the name as though it were a piece of bad fish.

The princess was silent for a moment. "It is sad," she said. "Very said. They are deprived of beauty."

"If Councillor Kornmuse continues to enjoy such success, we will all be. I may take refuge with the whiskheads myself, Your Highness, barricade myself in my own building." He picked up a glass paperweight. Examining it, he murmured, "And stifle my irritation with their clumsy verse and naive rhetoric."

He brought the bauble close to his eye. "Eastern," he announced, "fifth century. Very fine. Probably made with child slave labour of course, in that province, in those days, which is a shame. They say thousands died of starvation and torture. Still, very fine."

He held it up to the light and muttered, as if to himself, "And I would regret my privacy, and possibly a lack of soap." He sighed. "I grow too old for this art." He put the glittering sphere down on the princess's desk. It caught the light and flashed the same glowing amber as the glass-filtered light in the whiskhead boy's room that night. Jan.

Juliana quivered and tore her eyes from the globe. "Well, I'll just have to invite the whiskheads into my castle. So they can enjoy, as we can, the . . ." She found herself blushing as she spoke, and trailed off. She was thinking of Jan in her quiet garden, his pale arms in her rock pool.

The architect was faintly smiling. "I don't think, Your Highness," he said gently, "that it would be possible to invite them all into your home. It is a large home, but not large enough. And you too may notice a distinct lack of soap among your guests."

"How many of them do you think there are?"

He shrugged. "Two, perhaps three thousand. It is a very popular movement with the young people of the city."

She was silent. "Thank you, Master Crivello. Thank you very much."

🙟 ONCE HE HAD LEFT — without bowing quite as much as was customary, she noticed — she sat in the afternoon light from the embrasure, patterned by the serpentine wire grille. She was thinking of Jan's patterned chest, the musky candlelight of his room, and she grew warm and drowsy.

She flinched as the doors opened and a factor announced, "Lord Lucas of Carsenoud," and Lucas strode in behind him, his blond hair flying. His face was flushed with exercise and sun, his hand on the pommel of his sword.

"Juliana, are you — good God!" He stopped short, his smile vanishing. "What on *earth*."

"Oh. It's just a haircut, Lucas."

Lucas sat heavily, his long legs sprawling across the patterned stone floor. He squinted at her. "Are you all right? I thought we'd see you at Erika's last night. What happened to you?"

She smiled and looked down. "Sorry. I've been busy. I suppose I should have sent a message. Was she offended?"

"Offended, no, not really. I was just . . ." He averted his gaze. "Worried, I suppose. I wondered if you might be ill. You're not ill?"

"Not at all. I just hope I wasn't rude. I should have sent a message."

"Oh, I shouldn't worry. It was quite a large party anyway. Very gay, in fact, you would have enjoyed yourself." He frowned again. "What's this all about?"

"What's what all about?"

"Your beautiful hair! What got into you?"

"*Lucas* —"

"You look positively popular. You remind me of those young toughs who hang about those old buildings."

"Old buildings? Lucas, those are . . ." She sighed. "Never mind. You say I look like one of those children? Good."

"Good? Someone might mistake you for a whiskhead." His laugh echoed like a shot on the stone.

"That's the idea."

"Oh, for God's *sake!*" He rose, and began to pace. "Juliana, don't get carried away by some fashionable nonsense." He turned to face her, flushing. "I forbid you to experiment any further with this fashion. It is dangerous. They are dangerous."

"You forbid me?"

"As a friend. A close friend."

"Thank you, Lucas, for your protection. But you needn't worry. I have an interest in the whiskheads' fashion. A curiosity. Let's call it sociological. But that's all. I'm in no danger of being swept away by them. Besides, they wouldn't have me."

The young earl was pacing again. "Whiskheads. Everyone talks about whiskheads as if they're some . . . as if they're so damn interesting."

"They are."

"No, they're not, Juliana. They're not. They're dangerous and, and, and irresponsible. All they care about is their pretentious poems and art and their own pleasure when there are people suffering out there, people without adequate —"

"Suffering!" said Juliana hotly. "What do you know about suffering? And besides, they don't think only about their own pleasure."

"Oh they don't?" He sat again. "And what do you know about *that*?"

She hesitated. "They think about beautiful things. Which isn't purely selfish, it's something, something that benefits all of us, it's something . . ." She struggled to find the words.

Lucas dropped his mouth open dramatically. "How does it benefit all of us? Those useless and dangerous structures are a menace. They're unsafe. Furthermore, they are highly impractical for a modern city."

"What are you talking about?"

He waved a hand. "It's architectural and complicated. You don't have to worry about it. But, basically, my engineers tell me that the foundations are absurdly deep. You can't get a modern sewage system around them. There's no way. It's ridiculous. They should have thought of that when building them. Several of them will have to be destroyed. Anyway, I —"

"Several what?"

"The Architectons. The oldest ones will have to go. There's no way we can —"

"*What?* Destroyed?" Now she was standing. "Don't you dare. Lucas. Listen to me. Don't you dare."

He smiled and shrugged. "Juliana. Please. Calm down. These are architectural issues about which you know nothing."

Juliana clenched her fists. She knew her face was prickling hot, and that blushing always seemed to arouse amorousness in men, for strange reasons, and she hated herself for it and Lucas for sitting there smiling lasciviously at her, positively *leering*.

The other irritating thing about him was that he was right about the sewers. Something had to be done. And being so sensitive about the poor, in a way that, truthfully, few of his friends would even comprehend, he was succeeding in making her feel guilty. It was almost attractive.

Lord Lucas rose and moved behind her desk to stand next to her. He put an arm around her shoulder. "Listen —"

"Look," she said, "it's pointless to talk about this."

"Certainly," he said. He released her and sat on the edge of the desk. He began admiring his own forearms, flexing and relaxing them absorbedly. Juliana watched them too, reminded once again of Jan's pale arms, so much thinner. She shivered.

Lucas looked up at her and smiled. "Stiff," he said.

"From archery. I didn't shoot much all winter."

She smiled distractedly and sat again. He rose and moved behind her. Her neck bristled as she felt his fingers on it, lightly stroking the fuzz on her nape. "You're furry now," he said softly, "like a little animal. I could grow to like it."

She pushed his hand away.

"Listen," he said, close to her ear, placing both hands on her shoulders. "You've done enough work today, and it's warm. Let's go for a walk in the woods."

Again she shrugged off his hands. "Lucas, no," she said with fatigue. "Don't start that again. That's all over. Don't be silly."

Lucas laughed, and slipped off the desk. "You're right," he said. "I know you're right. Well." He was pulling on his riding gloves. "I'd best be off."

⟅ THAT NIGHT, ALONE IN HER humid garden, she stripped naked under a tree and covered herself in scented oil. She kept seeing Jan's face, and heard his condescending voice. She clapped her hands with anger. Then she slipped into her deep black rock pool, and in the cool of the water she was calm.

In her bedroom, she dried herself slowly and thoroughly with a thick towel.

FIVE

RINCESS
JULIANA
LEANED AGAINST
THE BAR AND WATCHED
the stage and the trap door
entrance to the whiskheads'
hall. Her hair was cropped
even shorter now, and that afternoon she had dyed it purple, with real dye, dye that would last for weeks. She was
proud of herself for finding the hall so easily in the
labyrinth of the great Architecton. Now she was reward-
ing herself with a tankard of thick, black kaash. It tasted
gritty and pungent, faintly rotten. It was making her
stomach churn.

It was still early, but already there were three
whiskhead boys near her, the wires dancing about their
ears. Occasionally they smiled politely in her direction
and she smiled back.

There was no music tonight, no performance. She
was unlikely to see Anton or Elisabeth. But there did
seem to be more young people arriving every half-hour,

occasionally whiskheads. At eleven it was almost crowded, and her legs were tired from standing. A whiskhead boy was sitting in a corner playing a folk song on a hand-carved holtor, and a girl she had seen before — the red-haired girl from the night of the performance — began dancing alone on the floor, barefoot. Her friends clapped for her.

Juliana's heart beat faster as she watched. She remembered that the girl had known Jan. Juliana's eyes kept darting to the entrance. She had not been prepared to be nervous; she was surprised that she was. She felt like leaving.

She took a deep breath and turned back to the bar, where she ordered a small jug of kaash — her last for the evening, she told herself, if Jan did not arrive.

She paid for her drink. Turning around, she bumped someone who was crowding her from behind, a tall man. "Sorry," she said, and looked up into Jan's face.

"*So* sorry," he said, bowing slightly.

The princess laughed and blushed and laughed again. "Hello," she said. He was smiling. She ran her eyes over him, his clean cotton smock, the curls at his neck. He put his hand on the bar next to her, gesturing to the bartender. She looked at the blond hairs on his wrist. She said, "Let me buy you, let me buy you something."

"Thank you," he said, "it's not necessary." He spun a coin onto the bar and picked up his jug.

"I'm glad I — I'm happy to see you."

"Yes?" He turned from her, looking at the dancing girl, waving to friends.

"Are you happy to see me?"

He paused, sipping kaash. Then he looked her in the eyes. She could smell soap and his skin. "Yes. Yes I am." He put a hand on her shoulder, his fingers grazing her neck, then quickly withdrew it and looked away again.

A boy with a drum and a girl with a tambourine had joined the boy with the holtor, and several people were dancing.

"Why don't we dance?" she said suddenly, and took his hand.

He let himself be led through the crowd. She took both his hands and they danced, clumsily, among the bare feet. Juliana tried to remember the steps of folk dances she had learned as a child, and trod on his feet. He laughed and held her closer to him so she could feel his warmth and smell his neck. She ignored the gazes of his friends, and the red-haired girl in particular, who smiled at her in a way that Juliana was not sure she understood.

But by the time they were both perspiring, the whole dancing crowd was perspiring, and the candlelit room danced with the vanishing flashes of wire ends, glinting about their heads, and nobody was looking at anyone else with anything but joy. Jan leaned forward and kissed Juliana on her shining forehead, and she laughed and put her hands around his waist. Breathing heavily, they pushed their way back to the bar and were silent for a moment. Then Jan took her hand and said, "Come."

⪻ IN HIS GAUZY ROOM, the glass bubble in the air, Juliana fell onto the bed and he fell on her, kissing her neck, his hands large and gentle on her breasts. She pulled off his shirt and laid her cheek against his chest. She ran her hands over his shoulders. She took his nipple between her teeth. She straddled him and pulled her shirt off over her head, then lay on him, their naked chests hot together, their nipples touching. Lightly, as lightly as she could, she stroked one of the wires protruding from his ears. He closed his eyes and moaned and quivered, his toes curling and uncurling like a cat's. She said, "Jan, I want you to trust me."

He said, "All right. I trust you." He rolled over so they were side by side, and he cupped her breasts in his hands.

Breathing fast, she said, "I want you to come with me."

"Where?" His voice was muffled because he was kissing her breasts.

Gently, she pushed his face away, lifted it up to hers. "To my place."

"I would love to." He took her nipple in his mouth. His groin was warm against hers.

"I mean now."

"Now?"

"Yes." She sat up. She looked at him looking up at her and smiled. She stroked his hair. "Come to my house. I want to show it to you. We can continue this. There."

He reached up and stroked her hair. "In a bit. Not now."

"Yes. Now."

"Why?"

"Trust me."

He rolled onto his back. He looked at her. "Why leave here? Is it not beautiful here?"

"It is. But I want you to see my place."

"Is it as beautiful as this place?"

"Are you afraid that it is?"

"Perhaps. Is it?"

"I don't know. That's for you to decide."

He smiled. "All right." He sat up, reached for his shirt. "Let's go."

THEY EMERGED FROM THE BASE of the Architecton onto the deserted square. The night air was cool. Scraps of paper blew over the cobblestones. There was a distant clatter of horses' hoofs from the streets around. "We'll take a cab," said Juliana.

"I can't —"

"I have money."

They left the square, and on a merchants' street Jan hailed a horse-drawn cab. "Now there is one condition," said Juliana, as they climbed inside. She pulled a silk scarf from her pocket. She wrapped it around his head, covering his eyes. She tied it tightly.

"Why? What are you afraid of?"

"Nothing," she said softly. She whispered in his ear, so close her tongue tickled him, "Trust me."

He sat back in the dark cab, his hand on her thigh.

She leaned out the window and curled her finger at the cabman, who leaned to hear her whisper.

🙥 THEY TOOK A CIRCUITOUS ROUTE. Juliana instructed the driver to take as many turns as he could, and to double back on himself. Jan said nothing. His wires hummed faintly in the moving cab. They came to the servants' entrance at the rear of the castle. She paid the man and guided Jan to the ground. Holding his hand, she led him inside and through the narrow passages and up the dark stairs to her quarters.

In her private garden, sweet with the smell of green, she removed his blindfold. It was dim. He said nothing as he looked around. He studied the drooping trees over the stone pool, the vines tangled around the pillars of the cloister, their purple blossoms. He started as an orange bird cawed sharply and fluttered away from him. Princess Juliana lit candles and brought them to the edge of the water. He walked to the edge of the pool and stared at the black surface which shimmered only barely with flame, still almost as a mirror. He looked at her soberly, his eyes wide. "Where are we?"

"At my house."

"You are very wealthy."

She said nothing.

"Are we in a great merchant's house? Or a noble lord's?"

She shook her head.

"Are we in Stjornokh or far away?"

She smiled and shrugged.

He put his hands on his hips. "We walked up many stairs. We must be in Goldenburg. Or a suburb. In the walled village past Outer Stjornokh."

"Shh." She stood up. She held out her hand to him. He took it and followed.

She led him down another corridor, away from her room and the outer walls. She avoided any window he could glance out, any archway where the royal coat of arms would be displayed. She led him to her father's library, where the wire-bound books were kept. She lit a torch and he fingered the volumes silently, watching the light dance on the filigree, intricate as organic growth. She opened a glass cabinet to show him the stone that glowed with a burning light, like a dying candle. He held it up, looked at it from all angles. There seemed to be an actual flame in the centre of the stone, moving sluggishly, like a flame in a dream.

"It's cold," he said with surprise.

She laughed at him. "Of course it's cold. It's a stone. It's a trick of the light. Phosphorescence. It was a gift from the wandering tribes of the East."

"To whom?"

"Come. There's something else."

She led him to the hall where there was an eerie sound, a whistling like distant singing. One vast rose window glowed, its thousand panes a thousand colours. The stonework that held the panes was so fine it appeared to be broken up, held in place by the glass itself. Jan held his hand in front of the window to feel a breeze. The ghostly singing rose and fell, subtly changing pitch. "There is a wind," he said. "The window is pierced."

"Look more closely. There are fine openings in the stone. See? And cracks here where the glass doesn't fit. The wind from outside passes through and makes the whistling. The window sings. It was made by a musicologist, a hundred years ago."

Jan stared at the window, holding his hand out into the breeze. "But there is no wind tonight." He looked at her. "We must be high up."

She took his hand.

"It is beautiful," he said solemnly. "All of it. I wish . . ."

"Yes."

"I wish there were more, more educated people. Like you."

"I am lucky to be educated."

"Yes. And they want to, to suppress it, to . . ." He was making vague shapes in the air with his hand. "They don't understand. They don't want it, they would replace art with brick boxes and citizens' committees."

"Who would?"

He shrugged. "The government."

She looked away and down. "I don't know," she said faintly. She took his hand again and turned. She led him back, through the inner corridors and up a narrow staircase, to her quarters. She led him through the garden, past the stone pool, to her bedroom. She had covered her windows with heavy rugs. She fell backwards onto the bed, and he fell with her, his mouth on her neck.

~ MOVEMENT BESIDE HER AWOKE the princess: she opened her eyes to grey light in cracks around the curtains. It was just before the dawn. Jan was not in the bed. She sat up quickly. He was standing, naked, beside the bed, as if he had just risen, looking around him. Quietly, on his soft feet, he moved towards the windows.

"Jan," she said sharply, "don't look out."

He hesitated, his hand on the curtain. "Don't worry," he murmured. "Now I trust you."

"No. Jan, I must —"

But it was too late. He jerked back the rug and it fell from the window. He stood in the narrow arch in the grey light. He drew in his breath sharply. He stood paralysed, looking out over the entire city, the soaring central Architecton in the distance, the smaller emerald spire to his left. He leaned forward, fingered the carved rosy stone around the casement. He stuck his head out and surveyed the castle walls. Then he pulled himself back in, folded his arms, and turned to face her. His face was contorted, with rage or fear, Juliana could not tell.

"Jan," she said, "I didn't want you to —"

"Don't speak to me."

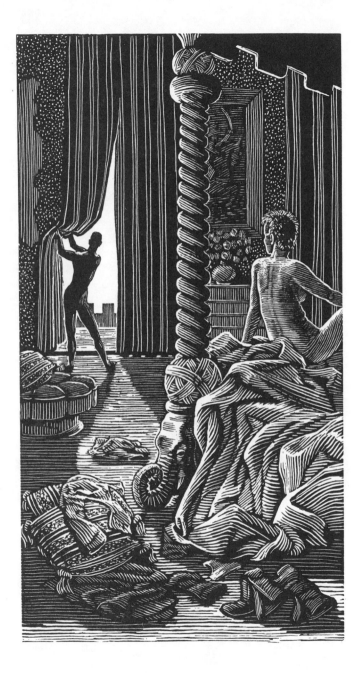

"Why not?"

"I know not who you are."

She was silent, staring at him.

He cocked his head and stared longer at her, and then he exhaled at length. "Sweet God," he whispered. "You are."

"Yes. But I didn't want to, I mean I didn't want to be. Who I am. With you."

"You cut your hair."

"Yes."

"To trick me."

"What?"

"To trick me and the others." He was gathering up his clothes, angry. "You disguise yourself to lure me, a peasant boy, to lure me here —"

"Oh, Jan, stop it. Stop it. Wait. Let me explain. I wanted you to see —"

"Do you do it often? What do you do with us afterwards? I know. I have heard what goes on at the castle."

"*What?*" She slipped out of bed, tried to restrain him. "Wait. Please. I don't know what ridiculous rumours you have heard. But they are not true."

"I can't be here. "

"All right. Leave. But don't leave angry."

"You lied to me." He was dressed now, looking around for the door. "How do I leave?'

Juliana sighed. "If you must, I will accompany you. But talk to me."

Jan refused. As she dressed, he sat silently at the casement, looking out at the sun rising over the city, the columns of smoke rising from rooftops. She put on a white nightdress.

All the way down the winding stairs, he would not speak to her.

"I never lied to you," she kept saying.

But he would not respond. He muttered that his brothers and sisters would never forgive him if they knew he had gone voluntarily to the castle, to be with the saviour of the citizens' committees, the sweet, noble, pure princess herself. And he had let her in, into his own secret place, his own private place . . .

She opened the secret door for him, and he stepped into the dewy grass behind the castle. A narrow path between bushes led around the walls. She stood in the doorway in her bare feet, hugging herself in her thin dress, and said, with anger in her voice, "What have I taken from you?"

He was already several steps away. He stopped and turned to her and said, too loudly, "You — you —"

"Step back!" shouted a male voice.

Jan spun to see a tall man emerging from the bushes. The man struggled with brambles and almost fell on stepping forward. He ran at Jan and tried to tackle him, but Jan twisted like a snake and darted aside; the man fell heavily. He rose, groaning, and said in a strong voice, "Stay away from her, you thug."

"*Lucas!*" hissed the princess. "*Lucas. Leave him alone.*"

The young earl and the peasant faced each other with clenched fists. Lord Lucas's face was grey and unshaven, his hair matted; there were twigs stuck in it. Juliana stepped between them, putting her hand on Lucas's arm. "Lucas, stop this. Stop this instant. What are you doing here?"

"I knew he would have to come out eventually. Are you all right?"

"Is *she* all right?" growled Jan. "How do you know *I'm* all right?"

"*What* is going on here?" said Juliana. "Have you been —"

"Are you all right?" said Lucas, gripping her arm and staring into her eyes.

She shook him off. "Of *course* I'm all right. Now what have you been doing here?"

"I saw you go inside," said Lucas. "With *him*. I knew you had been doing dangerous things but I didn't think you would go this far. I saw you leave the castle in your ridiculous getup last night. I was here when you arrived home with him. I wanted to make sure . . ."

"What? Make sure of what, exactly? You've been waiting outside all night? In these bushes?"

Lucas brushed at his face.

"To make sure I'm all right?"

"Yes."

Jan snorted. "Don't trust him."

"Listen, you," said Lucas, raising his hand, "I hope for your sake you have not touched her."

"Lucas, *shut up*. I am *perfectly* capable of looking after myself. Both of you, *stop* it. You — *you* have been *spying* on me." She shivered. Her feet were cold in the wet grass. "And *don't* pretend you were concerned for my safety. You wanted to know if I would spend the night with him. Didn't you? Well, I did."

Lucas stepped around her, towards the blond boy. "If you touched her, if you so much as touched her—"

"What?" said Jan, bumping his chest into the lord's. "Then what? Should I be afraid of you?"

They began pushing each other, while Juliana tried not to shout. "Stop it *this instant*. You'll wake someone."

Jan took a wild swing at Lucas's face and missed. Juliana let out a yelp and stepped out of the way. She put her hands over her face; she knew that to punch wildly at Lucas was a mistake. Jan was a gentle boy; she had found that out. And whatever experience he had in the streets of the city and the graffitied corridors of the Architectons she knew was no match for the noble lord's lifetime study of classical pugilism, his training with the best boxing masters of the royal court. Before Jan had regained his balance, Lucas had landed two deft blows quick as birds, one to the jaw and the next to the nose. Juliana heard the sickening crack as the cartilage broke, and Jan fell, clutching his face. She shrieked.

"All right," said another man's voice. "All right, that's enough."

From the bushes on the other side of the path emerged another dusty man, this one in black clothing, with a stooped back.

"Bostock?" said Lucas.

"*Bostock!*" The princess was kneeling at Jan's side, trying to get him to remove his hands from his face. "Let me see," she was saying. "It's all right. I can get you a doctor." The boy was quivering. "Bostock, not you too?"

"Leave him now, Lucas," said Count Bostock of Ivor, pushing Lucas backwards. "It's over. You've won. Yes," he said to the princess. "I'm just as ridiculous as he is. I saw you enter as well. I didn't know *he* was here." He kneeled at the side of the injured boy. "And I think that we should congratulate this young man, instead of wounding him, don't you, my friend?"

Jan scrambled to his feet, brushing off both sets of helping arms. His face was streaming blood, and there was dust on his forehead from his fall. He stood unsteadily. "Leave me be," he said between gritted teeth. There were tears in his voice. "Was this part of your entertainment, as well?" He turned and ran down the path, stumbling as he fled.

"Jan!" wailed the princess after him. But he was gone.

Lucas and Bostock were silent. Juliana turned her eyes on them, trembling. "Well," she said quietly. "Thank you. Thank you for all your help. You." She spoke deliberately, closing her mouth between each word. "You. Are.

Children." She took a deep breath. "Jealous. Little. Children."

"I'm sorry, Princess," said Lucas. "I thought he —"

"Get away from here. You had no right to injure him. He is a gentle boy. He is my lover."

Both Bostock and Lucas looked at the ground. "Princess," said Lucas, "it was only for your —"

"Get away from here. Get out of my sight."

Lucas picked up a riding glove he had dropped. Head bent, he strode away.

"Well," said Bostock gently. He touched her shoulder. "We are both ridiculous. In trying to be close to you, we both lose your esteem."

Juliana shrugged him off. "It is I," she said, with constriction in her throat, "who lose the most." Tears welled in her eyes.

Bostock nodded sadly. He swallowed hard. He looked pale in the morning light; there were black circles under his eyes. "If there is anything I can do to redeem . . ." He stepped towards her to put his arm around her shoulder.

Again, she brushed him off. "You too. I don't want anything you can give me."

"You are very upset. Permit me to —"

"Get away," she barked. "Go."

Count Bostock nodded. He shuffled away, his limp more pronounced with fatigue. She watched his asymmetrical shoulders bob out of sight along the path, then let the tears stream down her face.

SIX

T WAS
UNFORTUNATE
FOR JULIANA THAT
THE NEXT DAY WAS A
busy one. It was this day of
every month that she sat in
state from morning till afternoon, reading the bills proposed by her governments, by the Diet of Lords and the municipal government; she even had to acknowledge suggestions from the Convocation of Commoners. She sat at a table in a great hall of the castle, flanked by advisors, and read and talked and did her best to concentrate on the minutest details of school funding, road building, and the question of pensions for the palace guards. No one commented on her hair, the colour of quine wine, but they all stared.

By mid-afternoon her face was pale, and she rubbed absently at her furry head, as if to remind herself that her tresses were gone.

The very last statute brought for her approval was Lucas's long-awaited sewage reform: "A Bill to Institute a Hygienic Sewage System in the Capital City." She stopped yawning and read it carefully.

Officer Bude was at her side, his feather pen and bottle of ink and the royal seal at the ready. Once she had finished reading, she looked up at him, frowning.

"I trust," he murmured, lighting the stick of wax that would provide the seal, "that Your Highness approves?"

"Put that out, Officer Bude," said the princess. "I wish to read it a second time."

There was an uneasy silence as she read it a second time, then a third. She pushed the document away and rubbed her eyes. Then she yawned. Officer Bude was lighting the sealing wax again when she announced, "I veto this bill."

This time the silence was worse. Seven white heads at the table exchanged glances. Some smiled, expecting a joke. Carsenoud, Lord Lucas's father, murmured to his knights. Lord Elmflere shuffled papers. Officer Bude coughed demurely.

"Officer Bude?" said the princess.

"Your Highness," he began, "perhaps if you will permit me to explain some of the finer —"

"Thank you, Officer Bude, I need no further explanation. I understand the proposals fully. And I veto them."

"With respect, Your Highness, I hope you perceive the seriousness of the problems we hope to —"

"I understand everything, Officer Bude. I understand in particular that this bill calls for the destruction of three towers in the centre of our capital city, historical towers known as Architectons, whose foundations run too deep for the proposed sewage system."

The Duke of Carsenoud rose and cleared his throat. "The structures are in disrepair, Your Highness," he announced in the booming voice of a military commander. "They are perhaps even unsafe. And they are used for —"

"I know what they are used for, my lord," said Juliana evenly. "They are also great works of art. One of them was commissioned by my family, before I was born. And the —" She hesitated. "The people who inhabit them are also a part of our country —" There was open murmuring around the table. "A part of our *culture*, and as such important to *us*. But I am not sure why we are engaged in this *aside*, at the end of a long day." She spread her hands out on the table before her, raising them on her fingertips. "Perhaps I have been misheard. One moment ago I vetoed this bill. This ends discussion of the bill. Or am I incorrect in my procedures, Officer Bude?"

The advisor inclined his bald head.

"Thank you. Are we all agreed as to procedure?"

After a silence, a murmur of assent passed around the white-haired table.

"The bill is thus vetoed, the discussion is now ended. Now, I —" She paused, then repeated the word, as loudly as she could. "*I* will be pleased to inform *you* —

out of, I am sure we all agree, mere *politeness* — of the reasons for my decision. Sit down, Bude." She rose, and her lords and knights and councillors and advisors turned their faces up to her.

She spoke at length about her country, their city. She reminded them that respect for art was a Liralovian tradition — one which, they would all agree, clearly distinguished them from their neighbour, the cruel and contemptuous industrial state to the north. She instructed her lords and advisors to draw up a bill allocating funds for the repair of the major Architectons. She allocated several chests of gold — the same amount of gold that was to go to the sewage construction — to a fund for rebel architects, Master Crivello's coterie, which was still designing useless models of experimental shapes. She reminded Bude that she still had not been presented with the report on the activities of Councillor Kornmuse. She added an audit of Kornmuse's finances, for good measure. Messengers scuttled from the room.

"Now," she said, "since we have finished the business of the day, I would like to introduce a new bill of my own. Officer Bude, take dictation."

The advisor unrolled his parchment, dipped his feather pen. His obsequious smile was gone. The white-haired heads around the room were bowed, some breathing stertorously. She noticed that her father, the old king, had slipped quietly into the room, and had sat, unnoticed, on a bench. He had folded his arms and was watching her intently.

She took a deep breath. "A bill," she dictated, "to banish banality."

In the half-hour that followed, Princess Juliana instituted Banality Free Zones in the part of the city bounded by the old walls. The architectural codes were to be drawn up by Master Crivello. In the entire kingdom she prescribed a list of expensive building materials — the stones with which the old capital and her castle had been built — which were to be used in all new construction. She banned cheap materials. These statutes were to be law whether or not they were approved by the Diet of Lords or the Convocation of Commoners.

"My lords," she said as she stood. The entire room rose to its feet. "Thank you."

She moved through the crowd of bright robes, white heads bowing as she passed. At the door, her father was waiting for her, a crinkled smile on his face. He took her arm and patted her hand. They left together, and some said the king was seen to be chuckling.

🦅 "MA'AM," SAID OFFICER BUDE, the next afternoon. He clutched his hands together tight. A vein bulged on his forehead "Your Highness. A matter of some importance."

She looked up from her papers. "Mmmm."

"It has come to our attention, Highness, that there is some unrest in the capital. Some serious unrest."

The princess listened as he gave his report. She did not ask how Bude had gathered his information; she preferred not to know. And for once she was grateful for his rumour mill. It appeared that wild stories were spreading among the Convolutionists, and among the young who loitered in the market squares, stories that the princess of Liralove had disguised herself to seduce a peasant boy, only to have him beaten and tortured by men lying in wait. These stories had metamorphosed into tales of legendary sadism: some of the whiskheads believed that the princess had been "stealing" young men for years, and that some had never returned from the castle.

"Needless to say," continued Bude, "none of Your Highness's more recent statutes, those bills which she may proudly call *reforms*, has been implemented in so short a time. We are still making preparations. Of which the renegades —"

"The Convolutionists," she interrupted.

"Of which these people are doubtless unaware. What is most disquieting in this whole series of events . . ." He coughed. "What is most disquieting is that these beliefs have led to . . ." He paused, quietening. "Have led to talk of revolt." He raised his eyebrows high. "*Open* talk, Your Highness."

Juliana put her head in her hands. She thought for some time.

She said, "First, we must inform the whis — the Convolutionists, and indeed the entire populace, of what we intend to do. Perhaps these reforms will instill some confidence. Indeed I wonder why we do not make public our decisions as a matter of course, as soon as we have made them. Surely we have always done that?"

Bude coughed. "The parliament's wishes have always become known as they, as their laws —"

"From now on it will be our policy to print and post — immediately — our decisions throughout the kingdom."

"In this case, Your Highness, I fear it would be unwise to —"

"Make a note of it, Bude, if you please. New statutes. Published, posted, read in public squares. Immediately. Which means, if you recall, at once. You understand the immediately part, don't you, Bude? Good. Now. Second. I wonder why, in fact, my statutes have *not* yet been implemented. I see no reason for delay."

"No, Your Highness," said Bude hastily, "no indeed."

Juliana paused for a moment. Then she said, "I hope this works. I can think of nothing else to do."

Bude raised his eyebrows. "I would advise, Your Highness, some security measures in the capital itself. I could easily have an extremely powerful force at the ready in less than, say —"

"No, Bude," she said softly. "There will be no attacking the whiskheads." She rose, turned her back on him, and went to the window. She heard him shuffling out, not even bothering to cough.

🖎 SHE TRIED TO SLEEP EARLY that night, thinking the next day would be eventful. She spent a long while in her bathing pool and still, after drying herself very thoroughly with a thick towel, she could not lie still. She thought she heard voices, horses' hoofs, just outside her window, as if she were on a ground floor and not high in a tower. But when she rose and peered out her narrow window at the city, she saw nothing but a faint flickering of torches around the bases of the Architectons, just visible in the dusky light. The second time she rose, she realized that there was an unusual number of these lights. There was a glow in the central square. This was just after dark. She leaned far out her window and heard, carried on the still night, like the sound of distant waves, the very faint murmur of a crowd, cheering or chanting. Quickly, she wrapped her robes about her and went to rouse the officers of the Royal Guard.

A YOUNG CAPTAIN OF THE GUARD met her as she rushed down the winding stair. He told her breathlessly that a mob was approaching, a mob of youth from the city, carrying torches. They were several hundred strong, perhaps even two thousand, and some were armed with clubs. "We did not know, Your Highness," he finished in a rush, "how many of them there were."

Juliana bit her lip. It was no longer possible to avoid thoughts of a confrontation. She had to consider the security of all the inhabitants of the palace. She drew a deep breath and said, "Is the Guard ready to meet them?"

"Yes, Your Highness. A force of fifty horse has

mustered at the palace gates. Officer Bude himself has taken command."

"Officer *what?* Captain, run to them, and tell them to hold their attack. Tell them to wait for me. I am following you."

The young officer bowed and ran down the stairs, his sword clanging on the stone. Juliana shivered at the metallic sound; it was a noise she had never heard before so high in the castle.

She scampered down the stairs in her bare feet. Servants and officers were milling in the central courtyard, shouting orders, rushing about. They stared at her as she crossed the flagstones, with her dressing gown flying open to reveal her white nightdress. She strode through the main gates, and the lines of horsemen broke to let her pass through. Officer Bude, mounted, awaited her at the head of his column. He wore a helmet with the visor closed, and finely patterned armour which shone in the torchlight, his breastplate emblazoned with King Harvor's arms, the arms of Juliana's family. Juliana looked up at him, and he looked down through the slit in his visor. He did not look quite so ridiculous on his warhorse. Juliana looked around her, at the line of horsemen. They all wore chain mail and carried shields with the same royal arms. Juliana looked at their swords, the naked metal dull and ugly, and swallowed. Her heart was thumping so wildly she could hardly speak. Bude said nothing, but pointed his long sword downwards, to the road before them.

Juliana stepped forward and looked. Far below, a glowing sea of torches swelled outwards from the city gate. And as she looked, she heard the roar again, a sound like a song or chant, a phrase repeated by a vast crowd. She could not make out all the words. But one of them was "freedom."

She turned to Bude. "Give me your horse." She held out her hand for the reins. Bude made no move. His helmet was turned towards her, but she could not see his eyes through the slit in the visor. He sat silently.

The mounted officer to one side of him — a duke, Lord Camblerae, an old friend of her father's — lifted his own visor and stared at Bude in disbelief. "Bude," he barked. "The princess wants your horse."

Slowly, Bude dismounted, clanking in his armour. He almost fell as he tried to stand on the ground. Juliana vaulted onto the horse. Bude looked up at her, his gauntlets on his steel hips. She ignored him. She wheeled the horse to face her company. "There will be no advance," she announced, "until their force meets ours. We wait for them here." Her voice sounded high and frail in the night. The horses stamped uneasily. The duke, at her side, stared sternly at her small army as if daring them not to listen. She felt reassured and continued. "Then I will address them."

She wheeled again and watched the whiskheads march up the steep road to the castle gates. Their torches made them look like an advancing sea of light. The roar grew louder, the chant indistinct as they grew close; they were screaming hoarsely. From about two hundred yards away, they began to run at her. Her horse neighed and stamped, trying to move backwards, but she held him to his spot. She watched the whiskheads approach: hundreds of them, perhaps seven or eight hundred, perhaps a thousand. They were ragged and long-haired, mostly young men in peasants' shoes, but there were a few crop-headed girls in metallic clothing, their eyes wild with fright and anger. They carried pieces of wood and farm implements, hoes and poles. Princess Juliana raised her hand high to signal to her horsemen not to move, and to signal to the archers lining the castle walls to hold their fire.

The advancing whiskhead army slowed as they caught sight of the horsemen lined four deep at the castle gate. When the leaders had made out the strange sight of the young woman with spiky hair, barefoot, half undressed at the head of the horsemen, they stopped. The whiskhead force bunched up behind its front row, and there was a sudden silence as everyone stared at Juliana, her pale skin and white nightdress glowing in the night, the ranks of grey steel behind her.

Juliana cast her eyes over the whiskhead mob, a mob of children, almost all younger than she. They stared at her with confusion, their sullenness turning to awe. The points of light danced about their heads in the torchlight like a shower of sparks: the play of fine wires. She could almost hear them whirring. She scanned the crowd for Jan, but did not see him.

The princess stood in her stirrups and said, in a low voice that echoed off the ruddy stone walls of the castle and over the silent crowd, "We will not fight."

The horses behind her stamped and snorted, the armour and weapons clanked, but no one moved.

"We understand your anger. We want to help you." There were murmurs from the back of the crowd, jeers and hoots. But still the mob did not advance. "People among you have been spreading lies about what I did. I do not want to harm the Convolutionists, or change your lives. I do not want to prevent you from living in the Architectons. In fact, I have recently introduced a bill of law to save your dwellings."

She went on to explain the bill, the Banality Free Zones. As she talked, the crowd grew more restless. Those at the front could hear; they were leaning on their weapons and listening. Perhaps those at the back could not, for they began to shout. "Don't be fooled," they yelled, "don't be tricked." The crowd began to shift, to sway and swell as if the boys at the back were moving forwards.

The princess held up her hand once again. "We all believe in the same things," she said, as loudly as she could.

But her voice was being drowned. A chant had gone up from the rear of the group. "What about Jan!" they shouted. "What about Jan!"

Juliana was silent for a second. She looked at the ground and bit her lip. Then she announced, "I will prove to you that you are as welcome in this kingdom as anyone else. That what I have is yours. You will see for yourselves what we believe in. Lord Camblerae, open the gates."

The duke's eyes opened wide. He said nothing.

"Open the gates. I wish the Convolutionists to be welcomed into my castle."

A murmur of excitement went up from the whiskheads; she could not tell whether it was of pleasure or anger. Someone coughed behind her; she looked down to see Bude, his helmet off, his bald head glowing. He was peering up at her with anguish. "Please, Highness," he said, "no. It is very imprudent."

She turned her horse and trotted towards the castle gates, forcing the ranks of horsemen to part for her. "Open the gates."

A new roar went up from the whiskheads, and they surged forwards. The gates opened. The crowd flowed past the horsemen, into the courtyard, with Juliana at their head. She dismounted and was suddenly confused: the crowd was running past her, pushing and screaming; the castle guards were fighting with the whiskhead boys. She was spun around, then knocked over, and when she scrambled up, the courtyard was in chaos, jammed with bellowing people. Her horsemen had charged in behind her and were trampling whiskhead boys and shrieking cas- tle servants alike. A group of whiskhead boys had made it up a flight of stairs and were fighting with five footmen in royal livery in an open gallery on the second floor.

"*No!*" she screamed. "*Let me show you!*" She tried to grasp the shoulders of the youths as they streamed past. She tried to shout orders at the castle staff and the furious courtiers brandishing rapiers, telling them to let the intruders alone, so that they could explore the castle on their own. But her high voice was tossed by the noise. Her voice was like a streamer, lifted by the great clatter of voices and weapons and horses' hoofs, and carried up into the night air over the castle, where it dissolved.

She ran, in her bare feet, up the stairs to the open gallery where she had seen the fighting, in time to see the whiskhead boys breaking into the chapel where the Syllyrican ambers were kept, and many wire-bound books. She followed them inside and saw that they had stopped, were standing in silence in the chapel aisle, staring at the moonlight through the great stone tracery windows. She breathed slower. "You see," she said, "we have much in common. Let me welcome you into —"

She was interrupted by the thumping of wooden shoes and the harsh shouts of young men in the accent of the city: she turned to see a new group of young men arrive, dressed as labourers. She had just enough time to note that they were not whiskheads — probably, she guessed, the aggressive group who had been at the back of the mob, thugs who had joined the procession for fun — when they had pushed past her and were confronting the whiskhead boys. There was a lot of shouting. The new men shouted about privilege and luxury, and the whiskheads shouted back about art. The began to push each other, and then a glass-fronted cabinet broke and some books spilled out. "*No!*" she shouted. "Don't you see you are hurting yourselves!" But no one heard or looked. They were too concerned with breaking things. She could not watch any longer. She ran out onto the gallery and looked onto the melee below.

The whiskhead mob was fighting each other now, and soldiers were chasing them out with swords drawn. Glass objects fell from upper windows onto the courtyard floor, and she knew that one of the groups had got into one of the galleries. She felt sick and cold and could not move, her hand gripping the railing as she watched men and boys and young girls in hysteria, some of them breaking objects made by rural artisans hundreds of years ago.

And then she saw a face in the crowd she knew, a white bandage across the nose: a blond boy. He stepped between two fighting men, both intruders, tore them from each other and held them at either end of his long arms. He stood half a head taller than anyone else in the courtyard, besides the horsemen. Juliana's stomach heaved as she recognized Jan. He spoke sternly to the two men and threw them aside, then moved quickly to the next whirling knot of figures. The crowd was watching him as he separated fighters, calmed the chanting whiskhead crowd. The pushing in the courtyard was abating; Jan was convincing boys to gather around him and listen. They began to call their fellows back down from the staircases and balustrades.

And Jan turned his face up to where Juliana was standing. It was as if he had known all along she was watching him. He had a black eye. He held her gaze and she felt a mixture of shame and joy; she felt her face about to contort with tears. Quickly, as if a light had flickered on his face, he smiled. And just as quickly he turned away again. The next glimpse she had of him was standing on a stair, commanding the crowd in a booming voice.

Already some of them seemed to have fled, and the rest were panting, sitting or lying on the flagstones with their injured comrades and enemies around them. The Royal Guard had regrouped enough to herd some fifty whiskheads into a corner of the courtyard, where they cowered at lance-point.

The rest were listening to Jan. Juliana watched as if in a trance as he convinced all the whiskheads to reassemble in the courtyard, then negotiated with the Guardsmen to release their comrades.

The revolt could have ended here. Juliana often thinks about this, to this day. She reimagines the scene: it tortures her. She sees it with few variations: seven hundred youths, exhausted and saddened perhaps, but alive; the whiskheads, led by Jan, slowly marching back down the dusty road to the town, where they sleep, the town sleeps, and the incident ends. But it could not end after this.

 HROUGH-
OUT THE MELEE
AT THE CASTLE,
THE ROYAL GUARD
was regrouping, sending
messages to all the noble cas-
tles of the region, indeed of
all Liralove, that a revolt was in progress and the princess
was in danger. Horsemen and footsoldiers, including the
private cavalry of Lord Lucas, and the loyal guard of
Count Bostock, were gathering around the castle. By the
time Jan had calmed the mob and led the youths back
outside the castle walls, Lucas and his hot-blooded men,
the athletic sons of wealthy men, had gathered on the
highway and had to be restrained from massacring them
all. It was in fact Count Bostock who intervened and
insisted that his troop escort the frightened whiskheads
back to the city. In this confusion, the princess lost sight
of Jan. Count Bostock's army disappeared, the
whiskheads in their midst, and a sad quiet settled over
the castle.

The princess felt that she must have been awake for days; in fact, the riot had ended as quickly as it had begun. It was only eleven o'clock. She called for Lord Camblerae and asked him to send his men into the city to keep the calm. She knew that the townspeople would have found out about the outrage to the castle and that the whiskheads would now be in real danger. She also asked Camblerae to send criers throughout the city, to spread the word that the princess was safe, the castle was unharmed, the whiskheads had left peaceably, and all good citizens should go to bed. The duke bowed and strode away to do her bidding.

Left alone, the princess wandered through the castle, helping servants who were righting toppled bookshelves, sending bruised chambermaids to the nurses for cold compresses. She picked up a knight's helmet and walked with it up and down the stairs, too exhausted and dazed to decide what to do with it. Her maid brought her some riding boots, so that she would not continue to walk through the broken glass in her bare feet.

She finally retired to the eerie silence of her chamber. She undressed, her ears buzzing. Even after bathing in her smooth, dark rock pool, she could not sleep. She kept hearing the thundering of horses' hoofs around the castle walls, and wondered whose horses they were and who they were about to hurt and whether she had only dreamed them. She dozed and dreamed of shattering glass and the gleaming chest of a whiskhead boy who was made entirely of metal except for his wavy blond hair.

She woke in darkness with a start. Hours must have passed but it was still before the dawn. She could hear noise in the air, a distant roar like the sea. She rose, shivering, wrapped herself with a wool gown, and went to her window.

A column of fire rose from the city. Points of flame dotted the darkness, spreading outwards from the centre. She knew instantly it was her favourite Architecton, the one where the whiskheads gathered.

Within minutes she had once again woken the captains of the Royal Guard. Messengers, sent to her from the city police, confirmed that a large group of citizens of Stjornokh, thinking that a revolution was under way and hearing that the princess had been injured, had attacked the Architectons. Several were in flames. Whiskheads had been beaten; most of them were fleeing to the countryside or disappearing into the city's slums. The Guard assembled their horses and galloped into the city, into the bitter smell of burning wood, led by Juliana (who managed to dress this time).

They rode into the pall of smoke that filled the market square, where a sea of townspeople, perhaps two thousand, had gathered around the massive Architecton, bearing torches of their own. It was not difficult to disperse the crowd, since the worst was already over.

The people were quiet, having seen what they had done. The whiskheads had fled when the tower started to burn.

The tower had crumbled into a four-storey pile of beams and rubble. Fragments of paper whirled in the air like snow: the burned remnants of the whiskheads' posters, their bills and poems and musical scores. The crowd had stopped shouting: the citizens were staring at the flickers in the ashes with the faces of those who have woken from a dream and found it still night.

Indeed, the night itself was almost over: there was a cold glow in the sky. Juliana dismounted and stood for a long time watching the ashes. She sent the rest of the horsemen to patrol the rest of the town. But she could feel, and hear from the silence, that this eruption of non-Liralovian behaviour had subsided like a fever. As the sky turned grey with dawn and pale light washed over the buildings, the remaining crowd ebbed, slipping away into the surrounding streets. Many passing folk recognized the princess standing, a young guard at her side, amid the ashes. She looked upwards at the splintered beams, occasionally touching the blackened wood; they nodded, looked downwards, and hurried past.

She began to see other faces peering out of doorways, figures scurrying across the square to pick through the rubble in shadow: young people, in worn leather garb. Some of them, she knew, were whiskheads, their wires invisible in the pallor, hoping to retrieve some possession or paper before it was fully light. Soon there was a small crowd of them, walking among the ashes, not talking, picking up papers here, old shoes there. She asked one

young man if anyone had been killed in the fire; he bowed his head and held up four fingers. Four dead. He passed on. She did not know whether he had not recognized her or did not care.

Messengers from the Guard found her and told her that the city was quiet. Five Architectons had been burned to the ground, and the ruins had not yet been completely searched, but as far as they knew only six whiskheads had been killed. Some were badly beaten. The townspeople, now remorseful, had taken the injured in and were caring for them in their own houses.

The sun was rising behind the tall buildings of the square, needling rays between them. The sky was still pale, but Juliana could tell the day would be utterly clear, probably hot. A new crowd gathered to watch the whiskheads dig in the rubble; these were merchants, students, and other townspeople who had slept through the rampage, and now had come out to see what their neighbours had done. All of them had faces of shock and sadness when they saw the strength of the great beams that had supported the tower to the sky, the complexity of the vast joints that had held the vaults aloft, now thrown to the ground and scattered, uselessly splayed, as if by a giant angry child. Word began to spread among the crowd that many whiskheads had died, and some of the older women began to cry. Perhaps, Juliana thought, they thought of their own sons. She knew that none of them had ever known violence in their city, or even in their country.

A face passed across the square that caught her eye: a white bandage. She peered through two beams that leaned on each other to see Jan framed there, in a doorway. He stared at the crushed monolith like everyone else. He stood with a small whiskhead girl with shiny black hair. A new one. The sun glinted on the metal tattoos on her slim forearms.

Jan stared right at Juliana. She knew he had seen her, her hands on the two beams which met over her head like a roof, up to her ankles in smashed plaster. They stared at each other for a long moment. Jan nodded sadly, as if to say that there was nothing to say, and she nodded back. Then he smiled a grim smile, and put his arm around the small girl's waist. The girl leaned her head against his shoulder, and they turned and vanished down a narrow alley.

"Your Highness," murmured a voice behind her.

She turned, quickly wiping her eyes, to see a middle-aged man with a red face, who looked familiar. He was bowing nervously. Lucas stood at his side. "Juliana," said Lucas in a low voice, "you remember Councillor Kornmuse."

"Councillor Kornmuse. Of course. Have you come to gloat?"

"To gloat, Your Highness?" stammered the politician.

"Isn't this what you wanted? No more impractical architecture, the defeat of the immoral —"

"Your Highness —"

"Councillor Kornmuse," said Lucas, "wishes to make clear that he had no part in this uprising."

"I deplore it, Your Highness," said Kornmuse hastily. "I am just as deeply shocked as you. I had no idea that the people of this city would react so, so —"

"So violently."

"No, ma'am. It is contrary to my wishes. And indeed of all the right-minded —"

"All right, Councillor, spare us the right-minded citizens. I believe you. It doesn't matter now anyway. The destruction is done."

"Yes, ma'am." Councillor Kornmuse and Lord Lucas stared at the ground.

"And you, Lucas," said the princess. "I suppose you may go ahead and put your sewage system in. Are you pleased?"

"We came, actually," said Lucas softly, "to offer our support. To console you. We too are very sorry for what happened."

Juliana looked at the two of them, Kornmuse playing with the hem of his coat and avoiding her eyes, Lucas with his hands limply by his sides as if he no longer knew what to do with such weapons. They looked forlorn. "Thank you," she said.

They left in silence, and she saw a dark figure sitting among the ashes. A young man, expensively dressed, in black velvet breeches. His head was in his hands and his shoulders were convulsing. She threaded her way through the stones and put a hand on his shoulder. "Bostock," she whispered.

Without looking up, he put a hand over hers. She sat with him for a time, until he had stopped crying.

When they began to talk, they talked of odd things. Juliana's mind was empty from sleeplessness. He recited a sad poem by a famous Liralovian poet, verses which they had both had to study as children, about an unrequited love, the one that begins "I will dress you in poems white as wings," and has the line, "At the end of the day she is clothed in grey, and the evening silts away," which he knew would make her cry, and it did. She remembered that he had read her that poem when they were children, and he said he knew that she would remember.

They talked of their childhood for a while, and he finally said, "I was in love with you then." She said nothing, and so he said, "Which hasn't changed. I am always in love with you."

Juliana sighed and was silent for a long moment. She said, "I feel that you are my closest friend. Like a brother."

Bostock nodded grimly.

Then she said, "I admired you very much last night. For what you did, protecting those children. It was very brave."

He laughed tightly, and said, "That was nothing. That was nothing compared to what you did. When you opened the castle gates. Insane, perhaps, but very brave. And, most of all, it was very . . ." He paused, looking away from her pale neck, her blurry eyes under the red fuzz. "Compassionate. As usual. It was very compassionate."

Juliana was about to reply but started as a shadow loomed over them.

"Don't get up. I'm sorry to frighten you."

"Father!" Juliana and Bostock rose from the bricks they had been sitting on.

"Sir." Bostock bowed low, brushing the dust from his breeches.

The king was in common clothes, a riding coat and boots. A bodyguard in chain mail stood a respectful distance away, as if taking the air by himself. The king seemed to have entered the square unnoticed.

He embraced Juliana and made her promise that she was uninjured. "It took me a half-hour to find you in this mess," he said. "Everyone at the castle is looking for you. You will be interested to know that a number of messages have been arriving. From all the lords of the country. Camblerae, Anton, Hallerstam, Armstreme, almost all of them, and a lot of city councillors too, expressing support for your ideas. All of them endorsements of your proposed statutes. A special meeting of the Convocation of Commoners has been called for this afternoon. Your bills will be unanimously endorsed."

Juliana felt suddenly exhausted, and sat down heavily on her pile of bricks. "Excuse me," she said weakly.

He sat with her, took her hand. "You must be very proud."

She shook her head. "No, I am not. How can I be? With what I did to the castle — to your castle. I know how much you love the things that were broken. It was dangerous for you, as well. Where were you, when it happened?"

King Harvor snorted. "My cursed guards." He glared over his shoulder at the soldier waiting for him. "At first they attempted to restrain me. Said they weren't to let me out of my chamber. Because their orders were to protect me. Not let me *endanger myself*. Endanger myself! I told them I didn't know whose orders they were following, but if they thought those orders had greater authority than mine, I'd show them endanger. I had actually unsheathed my sword when they backed off."

"I am glad that they did."

"If they hadn't, I would have killed two of my own subjects."

There was a silence after this.

"By the time I got into it," the king said quietly, "the worst was over. Which is also fortunate, or I would have killed three or four of your young friends."

Juliana put her head in her hands. She felt a chill. She had forgotten that her father was a trained warrior.

"As it is, I think I only severely wounded one. I had him taken to the infirmary at once, of course. There are several still there. The nurses are with them." He paused. "I am sorry."

Juliana let out a sob. "I am sorry. I am so sorry. It was all my fault."

King Harvor put his arm around her shoulders. "Don't be ridiculous. Don't be silly. A few things were broken. Material things. They're not important."

She looked up, wiping her eyes. "No?"

"Not nearly as important as what you have done for the kingdom. How you have made people think. Besides, very little was hurt." He lowered his voice and said with a smile, "They didn't get the Flame in the Stone, or the Singing Window." He shrugged. "I have an idea, which I submit to you to use as you please. I would suggest you use this as a starting point. As an excuse to buy new art for the castle. You can commission it from the whiskheads themselves. And their craftsmen in the country. It will be a conciliatory gesture, and the time is right to convince Kornmuse and his people. They feel guilty enough to support it. And it has its economic effect as well. I was never opposed to aiding industry however we could. You remember when there was a bad grain harvest and we had to fund the farmers for a while, when there was the price war with the Gathians, and my finance minister wouldn't —"

"Yes, Father. I remember."

"You do?" He raised an eyebrow at her. "I didn't think you paid much attention in those days."

"No. I didn't."

"Yes. Anyway. These little boosts always . . . well they're diplomatic and they make work at the same time. I suspect the inhabitants of Stjornokh will want to see a gesture like this as well."

"I will do it without hesitation."

"You get the nobles in on it too, of course."

Bostock chuckled. "The thing to do," he said, "is to get them competitive about it. Who is the most devoted to art, sort of thing. Who awards the biggest commission."

King Harvor smiled. "I never did understand, Bostock, why you weren't interested in government. You have all the right instincts."

Bostock laughed, shaking his head. "I make no promises, sir. But I will set this in motion. It's the least I can do." He stood, and swept his arm around to take in the square and its ruins. "This building we shall rebuild. I will put up the money myself."

"Bostock!" said the princess.

"I will hold a competition for designs. There will be very strict rules. Nothing practical. Sheer uselessness. The most audacious design will win. I will advertise it across the land. I promise."

The princess smiled, then laughed, then felt tears flooding her eyes again. "It is the right thing to do, Bostock."

He ran his hand over her hair. "It is an easy thing to do. Your hair will grow back, do you know? I can feel it growing."

Juliana cried and laughed. She watched an old peasant woman push a wooden cart across the square. It was a food cart, with an urn of hot tea and a pile of buns: the first market stall of the day. She watched the woman stop the cart and unfold her stool. The smell of the fresh bread washed over the smell of smoke. Close behind the old woman came a group of four young men in country clothes, musicians with carved wooden instruments. They too were going to set up in the square, to busk. They spent a few minutes marvelling at the destruction, then they turned to the old woman and bought mugs of tea and buns from her. She joked with the troubadours, and Juliana heard them all laughing, a gentle sound that fell like rain on the ashes.

As the sun rose above the rooftops surrounding the square, more merchants arrived to set up their stalls. The troubadours finished their tea and began playing folk songs, at first quiet songs in a sad key, and then some dances with a mournful cadence. Juliana knew all the tunes. She breathed in the smell of the fresh bread.

Then she wrinkled her nose: there was another smell on the air, foul and swampy. It was the smell of inadequate plumbing, of sewage.

THE END

ABOUT THE AUTHOR

Russell Smith was born in South Africa and raised in Halifax. His first novel, *How Insensitive*, was shortlisted for the Governor General's Award, the Chapters/Books in Canada First Novel Award, and Ontario's Trillium Book Award. His second novel, *Noise*, received widespread acclaim, and a collection of short fiction, *Young Men*, was shortlisted for the Toronto Book Award. He works regularly with the CBC and writes for *The Globe and Mail*. He lives in Toronto.